MONTANA
Dreams

A Montana Romance

also by

velda **BROTHERTON**

Sexy, Dark, and Gritty.

Twist of Poe Mysteries

The Purloined Skull

The Tell-Tale Stone

The Pit and the Penance

Masque of the Rising Moon

The Victorians

Wilda's Outlaw

Rowena's Hellion

Tyra's Gambler

Other Titles

Beyond The Moon

Remembrance

A Savage Grace

Once There Were Sad Songs

Stoneheart's Woman

Wolf Song

MONTANA *Dreams*

A Montana Romance

VELDA
BROTHERTON

GALWAY

OGHMA CREATIVE MEDIA

www.oghmacreative.com

ISBN: 978-1-63373-233-9

Interior Design by Regina Hankins
Editing by Gil Miller

Galway Press
Oghma Creative Media
Bentonville, Arkansas
www.oghmacreative.com

To my daughter, Jeri

You always knew I could write and nurtured my need to do so.
Thanks, sweetheart.

One

Dessa leaned back against the hard seat of the lurching stagecoach and closed her eyes. Strands of long dark hair escaped from under her stylish blue hat and stuck to her sweat-dampened brow. Kansas City had been hot, but this... this incessant hot wind left her gasping for air. With a tired sigh she unpinned her hat and placed it in her lap, touched a fingertip to the bedraggled quail feathers. By the time they arrived in Virginia City, the hat would be ruined and so would she. What a dreadful trip. Who in their right mind would want to live out here in Montana Territory, anyway? Montana indeed. What was her father thinking?

The howling August wind puffed clouds of dust around the window shades so that she nearly choked with every breath. Perspiration ran between her breasts, soaked the stiff corset and camisole. She made a childish face and hooked a thumb under the fabric to scratch.

What she had seen of this horrendous wilderness during the brief stops since leaving the train station at Devil's Gate had not been encouraging. No matter what Mother and Daddy said, she would not stay one minute more than was absolutely necessary.

From a limp reticule she removed a fragile fan and waved it in front of her face. The effort only made her hotter and she dropped both hands into her lap. Despite the dust, she leaned over and rolled up the curtain on the far side of the coach to let in some air. Some choice. Choke to death or fry.

She was fastening the shade when a horse galloped into her line of sight, the rider stretched high in the stirrups. He wore a red bandanna pulled over his nose and a sweaty black hat crammed so low she couldn't make out his eyes. He held the reins in one hand, while the other waved a long-barreled pistol.

His shouted command was buffeted along in the turmoil of wind and swirling bits of debris and heat so that the words arrived disjointed and easy to disbelieve.

"Rein up, rein up there before I shoot."

From up top came a mangled reply, the fierceness of a battle yell, and the sharp crack of a whip. The stage lunged forward, and Dessa grappled frantically for something to hang on to. She bounced around in the empty coach, thunking up and down painfully. The wild and terrifying ride was punctuated by a couple of shots, a scream of agony, and shouted curses that set her heart thundering.

"Whoa down, you ornery cusses. Whoa down."

The stage rocked to a halt. Frozen with fear, she knelt on the floor, peering as best she could through a crack along the bottom of the window covering. Thank the Lord she hadn't opened both sides, or they'd see her for sure.

In the next breath she realized how foolish such a thought was. No one would rob a stage and not look inside. The realization gave her such a chill that her teeth rattled. Surely they would hear!

From outside came the snorts of horses; in her chest, the rumble of her own heartbeat. Her temples throbbed and intermittent flashes like stars flaring invaded her vision. This was a holdup, an honest-to-goodness holdup, and here she was right in the middle of it. She caught her breath and remained hunkered where she was. Maybe she could wish herself invisible and they'd just ride away. But then what? Suppose the outlaw had shot the driver and the man riding up top, the disgruntled one who was supposed to protect the stage with that fearsome-looking gun he carried.

She closed her eyes tightly, clenching her fingers together until they hurt. Nothing would happen to her. Surely. Surely, it wouldn't.

The door jerked open. She had pressed up against it so tightly that she almost tumbled out onto the ground. Teetering there, she sucked in a breath, afraid to look, afraid not to.

The bandit grabbed her. "Get down out of there, little lady. Come on, now, don't be shy."

He dragged her out by one arm and tossed her on the ground. She landed on her rear end, legs spraddled in a very undignified sprawl with the skirt of her blue dress hiked to show lacy, beribboned pantaloons.

To her horror both the driver and guard lay sprawled nearby, neither of them moving or making a sound.

"You…you killed them," she said.

The horrid man stood over her. "And you'll be next if you don't behave." His voice was raspy, his eyes cold and hard. Nothing like the romantic figures portrayed in the dime novels she read on the sly. This man's nasty manner was realistically threatening, and he stank like a sweating animal.

"Well, ain't you a fancy little thing?" a younger voice said from out of her range of vision.

Two of them. She was too frightened to look around, so she continued to stare at the scuffed, worn boot toes of her captor. Her daddy was right, she should have traveled with him and Mother. If he was here right now, he'd soon put these scoundrels down. As for that no-account buffoon they'd hired to accompany her, she hoped he rotted in that saloon in Devil's Gate where he was no doubt still drinking and gambling. Some reliable protector he was.

Now she would be killed out here in the middle of nowhere and no one would ever even find her bones. The thought made her more angry than fearful. Hadn't her parents been through enough, losing Mitchell in the war? Tears welled in her eyes and she sniffed.

Red Bandanna said, "Aw, look at this. You've gone and made her cry. Ain't you ashamed of yourself?" He grabbed her wrist, hauled her to her feet, and tugged at the ring she wore.

She jerked her hand away. "No, you leave that alone, you uncivilized animal."

He laughed harshly and tucked the long-barreled pistol into his waist. "What's this? Little fancy wants to fight. Well, come on, honey. I'll tussle with you awhile. Got nothin' better to do anyways. I want me that gold ring. Lookee there. What does that F stand for? Fancy? And look at these purty jewels. See 'em shine. Bet this is worth a lot."

Dessa thought her heart would leap from her mouth, and it probably would have except that her tongue and lips were so dry it just got hung in her throat. She couldn't even swallow or speak except to croak. The rank smell of the outlaw washed over her as he locked both arms around her shoulders and lifted her easily off the ground. This was worse than anything she could have imagined while lying on her bed back home reading Hurricane Nell or Bess the Trapper. This was too real, too dangerous.

"Coody, dammit, quit horsing around. I can't find the blasted money box. Leave that little gal be and get up here."

"I aim to tie her first. I'm taking this one with me."

"Yank'll have a fit."

"It's that or kill her, you lamebrain. You done called me by name and she heard you. How'd you like it if I just come right out and told her what you're called, too? Then she could go right to the sheriff with it. Like that, would you?"

"Holy cripes. Here's the blamed box, jostled tight up agin the rail with this bag over it."

He opened the offending leather satchel—her satchel—and dumped it. A stiff mountain wind grabbed at Dessa's clothing, sailing dresses and undergarments off into the stark wilderness in billowing clouds of color.

Tossing down the heavy metal box, the younger one jumped nimbly from the top of the stage. He let out a grunt when he landed, his worn boots sending up puffs of dust. "Do what you're gonna with that gal and let's get out of here 'fore someone comes along."

Coody hooted. "Yeah, like who? Give that railroad a little more time and won't no one be riding this trail. Won't no towns at all be in this godforsaken country. Won't even be no stages to rob."

While he talked, Coody unceremoniously bundled Dessa up under one arm and draped her face-down across the rump of his horse. He lashed her wrists together behind her, hitching up the leather thong so tightly it cut into her flesh. She bit her lip, refused to cry out.

The other one guffawed. "She ain't gonna stay on that way, you lophead. Start trotting that horse and she'll bounce right off into the dust. Apt to kill her. Here, let me show you."

The younger outlaw dragged Dessa off the horse and plucked at the knots of rawhide his partner had tied.

"Well, hell," Coody shouted, and jumped the smaller man. "You leave her be 'fore I swat you up the side a your head."

Dessa felt as if she were living in a nightmare. Yes, that was it. A dream. Only a hideous dream from which she would awaken and be safe and sound in her bedroom in Kansas City.

Her knees grew weak and she sank abruptly to the ground nearly under the nervous horse's belly. Long legs danced one way, then another, the large hooves barely missing her. She thought of the riding stable in Kansas City and the shiny, groomed gelding she rode every Sunday afternoon. A far cry from this disgusting, unwashed thing that suddenly let go a big smelly green splat almost on the hem of her dress and then gave a whinny that sounded like a laugh aimed directly at her.

Enough. Dream or real, she'd had enough. The men tussled with each other like overgrown boys. Without another thought for her safety, she scrambled to her feet and lit out running, shaking free of the loosened thongs to hold her long dress up out of the way of her ankle-high shoes. Gasping for every breath and afraid to look back for fear that big ugly man was looming right over her, Dessa sprinted through knee-high grasses and dodged scatterings of rock. But she was no match for the long-legged Coody. She heard his harsh breathing just before he latched one arm around her waist, lifting her so that her legs continued to pump air.

She jabbed at him with an elbow and felt a satisfying thud.

"Danged little hellion. You're just what I've been looking for," he panted, and tossed her without ceremony into a clump of bushes.

Up until the moment he covered her body with his, his tobacco-stained mouth sucking at her clenched lips, she had truly thought deep down inside that this wasn't really happening to her. It was, indeed, some kind of dream that she would awaken from before real harm could come to her. But then she looked into that dirty, pockmarked face and felt his stinking body mashing her breasts and stomach and thighs, and she knew it was real. Sick fear squeezed at her insides, and she tumbled mercifully into a black abyss of unconsciousness.

When she came to, she was riding behind the man, wrists bound together around his waist. The thongs had cut into her flesh until both hands were numb. Between her legs, the hot hairy hide of the horse chafed through the thin fabric of her pantaloons. He hadn't had his way with her. Not yet, anyway. She would know for sure if he had.

Her cheek lay against his back and she looked directly into the flaming ball of a setting sun. She closed her eyes, trying not to move and let the man know she was awake. Blessedly, the sun finally sank behind the ragged mountain peaks to the west. Then the horses turned and they were headed in the direction of the flaring orange and purple sky. She must have done something to alert her captor that she was conscious, for a chuckle rumbled in her ear and vibrated her body where it pressed against his.

"Little one's back with us. What we'll do, lad, is stop for the night up ahead in that wash. No sense in trying to get back in the dark."

Her heart tumbled all over itself.

"You just wanta roll around on the ground with that little gal, and you figger Yank'll take her away from you, we go on back to camp."

"Let him try," Coody said. The menacing tone was oddly tinged with fright, like the snarl of a wild thing threatened by a more powerful enemy.

'You say that now."

"Well, I'm stopping anyway. I ain't gonna get my mount's leg broke going over that mountain in the dark. Or my own blamed neck, either, for that matter. You do what you please."

The other man fell back to ride where he could study Dessa. She got a good look at him for the first time. He was little more than a boy, with fuzzy cheeks and a large hat that folded out the tops of his ears. She was reminded of a child playing dress-up. Everything he wore seemed to be too big. Briefly she wondered why he gave orders to the one he called Coody with such alacrity. Maybe they were brothers, or more likely he was just the smarter of the two.

The thought came to her that they were going to use her completely up and then kill her. It was almost a revelation; all of a sudden, the light dawned and everything was crystal clear. No one would come to save her. She had to do it herself or she would die, slowly and harshly. An uncontrolled whimper bubbled from deep inside, but she swallowed it down. If she was going to die anyway, she'd make a quick job of it, and they'd be sorry when it was all over.

At that moment the mountains devoured all traces of sunlight and glowed with a pearly pink halo. The ground became shadowy and indistinct.

"Here. Right here'll do," Coody said, and drew up his horse.

From somewhere nearby water flowed. Oh, God, for a drink. For just a few sweet drops to moisten her tongue, to trickle coolly down the back of her throat. She almost cried out with the need.

Coody sawed the thong off her wrists, unleashing an excruciating pain. She held her silence and bit at her lip to keep from crying out.

"Pull her off here, kid, so I can get down. I'll swear, I'm so thirsty I could drink cactus juice with the spines left in."

The young one held her a bit too long when she staggered around on her feet. "Please," she said, her voice sounding like dry husks of corn rubbed together. "I need a drink."

Fingers of one hand biting into her upper arm, he guided her beyond a darkening thicket toward the sound. At the stream's edge he unceremoniously shoved her forward. She landed on both knees. Gravel bit through layers of clothing to puncture her skin, but she paid no attention. Like a dog she leaned forward on both hands and lapped at the water, sucking in the icy cold snowmelt and gulping down great mouthfuls.

It hit the bottom of her stomach like heavy stones, rolled around there for a while, and started back up. She groaned and sat down right there in the creek, hugging her belly and rocking. In the rushing water shreds of the lovely blue dress boiled up around her.

Once the queasiness was under control, she cupped her hands and sipped delicately, stopping to wash her face and neck, then drinking again.

Coody finished his own noisy slurping and claimed his prize, dragging her out of the rocky stream and up the bank. She couldn't keep her feet under her, but he didn't seem to mind. The younger one he called kid had begun to pile up brush and wood for a campfire. Coody tossed her to the ground, and started flailing the boy around the head with his sopping hat. Curses of rage poured from him, and the boy threw both arms up to protect himself.

"How many damn times I got to tell you, take care of the horses first? Look at 'em. Carried us all day, sweating and hungry, and there they stand. Unsaddle 'em and stake 'em to that grass yonder. Let 'em drink some first. I have to run with such a idjit."

Coody wound down at last and the kid surprisingly did as he was told. Frightened by the outburst, Dessa moved backward into a thick growth of brush with dry, crackling leaves. It was dark there in the wash, but she could still see the shadowy outline of objects back the way they had come. Trees and outcroppings of rock humped blackly into the silver glow of the night.

She didn't really think about what she was going to do, or even consider her chances. If she stayed, this animal would have his way with her, and she would die before she let that happen. She had to try. As quietly as she could, she crept along in the darkness cast by the huge trees that grew on the creek bank. And all the while, all she could think of was the heartbreak of learning of Mitchell's death in the war, of the way Mother looked when she found out, as if her very reason for living had just flown out of her. The anguished gaze in both her parents' eyes when they heard news of her brother's death would remain with Dessa always. If she died here, what would it do to them? They lavished all their love on her—so much sometimes that she felt smothered.

At last her eyes grew accustomed to the darkness and she was able to make out an enormous pile of boulders at the foot of a rise. If she could reach the deepening shadows, Coody would have no idea where to look for her.

Every nerve in her body urged her to bolt for safety like a stampeding animal. She forced herself to measure the distance, judge her chances, and gauge the right time to go. Hair on the back of her neck prickled, chills tightened the muscles of her stomach, and her wet dress weighted her to the ground. Coody was still cursing the boy at the top of his lungs, his back turned to her. She had to do it now or not at all. It was time to move. She slunk away, hunkering low so she wouldn't cast even the vaguest of shadows when she left the shelter of the trees and headed for the rocks.

Crouched far back in the refuge offered by the immense boulders, she knew when he discovered her gone. The curses that had been aimed at the boy were turned on her. Vile, evil names he called her, shouting them into the night in a high, screeching voice. She made herself as small and insignificant as she could in the darkness of her hiding place. Though every ounce of her wanted to run as fast as the wind, she scarcely even breathed.

He couldn't possibly know which direction she'd chosen if she didn't make any noise. And luck might take him away from her; that's all she could count on. Luck. Her own, not his.

Coody stomped up and down the creek, his voice growing hoarse with shouting, before he finally quieted down. That was scarier than hearing him rage, for he might be sneaking right up on her where she hid among the rocks. She had to get farther away as quickly as possible, but she dared not move until he stopped looking. He would find her or he wouldn't; she could do nothing more but wait.

Despite being cold and uncomfortable in her wet clothing, Dessa finally dozed from pure exhaustion. She didn't know what woke her or how late it was, but a small fire flickered in the camp where the two outlaws now appeared to be sleeping, and their prey not five hundred yards away shivering with fear and chills.

For what seemed like an eternity, she stared at the two dark mounds that had to be Coody and the kid. Nothing moved or made a sound. Even the horses slept. How she wished she could sneak back into camp and mount up, ride like the mountain wind, far and fast and free. But that would be much too dangerous. Instead she decided to make her way around the point and head back in the direction from which they had all ridden earlier. Somewhere back there they had left the road, and once she reached it, surely she could find a town or a house or meet up with a traveler. If not, dying in the middle of nowhere in the brutal sun of the next day would be better than having that hairy man putting his hands all over her, defiling her body. She knew one thing for sure, the light of day would have to see her far from here. Come morning, if Coody decided to track her on horseback, he could ride her down in no time. She could only hope that the outlaw's need to return to camp with the stolen strongbox would be more pressing than his desire for her. His fear of the mysterious Yank was a palpable thing, and perhaps that would save her in the long run.

By the time the sky to the east silvered, Dessa's feet were burning with blisters, and the calves of her legs, unused to prolonged walking, were knotted. Arid throat locked closed, she watched with dread the rising sun, for it signaled another long, hot day. For a while she prayed for rain; then, seeing the uselessness of that in this parched land, she began to pray for the strength to survive. On she trudged, once in a while stumbling to her knees. After a moment she would rise again, but each time, she knew, might be her last. How much farther she could go, she had no idea. If she had reached the road in the night, she had missed its tracks, and so she could do nothing but head into the rising sun.

About noon, as she could calculate by the position of that ghastly burning ball crossing the white-hot sky, all energy seeped from her tortured body and she collapsed in the rocks and dirt and scraggly grass.

Just let me lie here a little while. Just a minute or two and I'll have my breath back, and then I'll go on. Please God, then I'll go on. And I'll get out of this awful nowhere place. There'll be a house with white sheets flapping on a clothesline and a stone well in the yard with a wooden bucket overflowing with cool, clear water.

The vision came to her so intensely that she imagined the smell of wet green grass and lye soap.

There will be kids playing out back, laughing and chasing each other, and their mother will come to the door and call out, "Mitchell. Dessa. Come in to supper now."

And the boy will stand straight and tall and look at me when I come up the lane to the house. The wind will blow his dark beautiful hair and his eyes, green like mine, will widen with recognition.

Tears trailed down her cheeks. She forced herself to rise, first to her knees, then to her feet.

"Oh, Mitchell," she sobbed.

The young boy beckoned, reached out, and faded into wavering ripples of heat.

She would follow, she would find him. She would not lie here and die. And so on she trod, marveling that after all these years, the youthful ghost of her dead brother had returned to save her life. The thought didn't seem at all odd. Mitchell's spirit had been with her since the day he left, and despite everything, she felt in the deepest part of her heart that he was alive out there somewhere.

When she told Daddy, he said, of course, Mitchell lived in her heart and always would. But that wasn't what she meant, and he wouldn't listen.

On and on she staggered, fists clenched around wads of her clothing in an effort to hang on to something. Stumble, fall, get up, and move on. Mitchell would have it no other way.

Afternoon came and went, the angle of the sun ever changing until at long last she felt the coolness of its absence and realized it had disappeared once again behind the mountains. And still she had found no road and nothing else, either. But blessed darkness, in the end, saved her, for no sooner had dusk melted into night than she spotted a dim glow off to her right. Someone had lit a lamp or built a fire.

She sobbed and veered toward the yellow pinpoint of light, stumbled, and fell. Counting how many times she fell and climbed back to her feet became a deadly game. Her time was nearly up, every ounce of strength almost gone. Soon she would fall and not be able to rise again. She tried to cry out, hail the house, but no sound save a croak could she force from her swollen throat. Surely she wouldn't come this far only to die within sight of salvation.

All she remembered after that final silent plea was crying out feebly, stumbling one last time as the door swung open and spilled out a long shaft of golden light. And her shouting and shouting and shouting. Then falling, only instead of hitting the punishing ground, she was swept into strong arms and carried, head snuggled against a muscled chest that smelled vaguely of coal oil and woodsmoke and leather.

The whiskery face she looked into when she regained her senses did not belong to the man who had carried her. This one was small and stringy and hairy, and he smelled of horses and tobacco. No, this was not her rescuer. But it didn't matter. She was alive, and oh, how wonderful it was.

The hairy man offered her a tin cup and she took it, wanting to gulp at the soothing water. His gnarly old hand stayed the impulse.

"Take 'er easy, now. A little more, and then wait. Don't want you sick on us."

She nodded mutely, accepted the sips as he offered them, and looked around the small room. Rough-hewn bunks, a long table and four chairs, a cookstove with a huge pot of something bubbling off steam, some shelves along one wall, and the window through which still shined the light that had saved her life. It came from a plain kerosene lamp. There were no delicate roses painted on the glass shade that had grown a bit smoky from an improperly trimmed wick, but that flickering glow was the most beautiful sight she had ever seen.

Men lived here. No woman's touch anywhere.

After yet another small sip of water, she mumbled, "Where—"

At the same time the grizzled old man asked, "Now what in the thunder is a pretty little thing like you doing wandering around in the night?"

Before she could answer, the door swung open. She cringed back into the corner of the bunk, desperately looking for a place to hide. Surely that horrible Coody hadn't found her already!

The old man gentled her. "Now, now. It's jest ole Ben Poole. He found you and brung you in. Now, little lady, it's jest ole Ben, who wouldn't hurt a flea, despite his size." The old man patted ineffectually at her arm, but she wasn't ready to calm down just yet. Not until the huge shadowy hulk came into the lamplight, not until she saw a head of shaggy blond hair, remarkably fine features, and the kindest blue eyes that must exist in the whole wide world. He had black lashes that made him look like he was wearing eye paint. How startling. How fascinating.

Embarrassed that she had stared, Dessa dropped her glance to the broad chest covered by a faded shirt open at the throat. The very place where she had rested her head while his strong arms carried her to safety

Hot tears spilled down her cheeks. The man said nothing, just settled his gaze in first one place, then another, looking not at her but around the cramped room as if he'd never seen it before.

"Here, now, young'un," the old man soothed. "You just lay yourself down and get some sleep. Everything will be fine come sunup. Ain't nobody going to hurt you. Ain't that right, Ben? Oh, by the way," he continued as he covered her right up to her chin with a threadbare quilt as if she were a child, "I'm Wiley. Wiley Moss, and this here's Ben Poole, but I done told you that, I reckon."

He must have had more to say, for she fell asleep to the murmur of the old man's voice, her gaze fixed on the broad back of the blond giant as he slipped from the cabin without ever speaking a word to her.

Two

Ben pulled the door shut at his back and stood there a few moments, eyes turned up toward the star-scattered ebony sky. A fingernail moon had set soon after dusk. Lucky for the girl. If someone was looking for her, moonlight would have been her mortal enemy. He sucked air down into his lungs and let it out slowly. Damn anyone who would hurt such a helpless little thing. He could hardly stand to look at her and think about it.

He shook his head and grinned at his own foolishness. This was the first time he'd ever gone plumb dizzy-headed over a woman. And at first sight, too. Never had known what to say to females anyway, but that just caused him to avoid most of them. Once his mouth opened, he felt utterly foolish, whatever came out. Maggie said it came from being raised up knocking around on his own without a mother. She always added that learning to kill when he was fourteen hadn't helped much, either.

He'd killed his first man at Gettysburg. Two years later, barely sixteen, he followed Lee out of Richmond in the last days, no longer knowing how many he had slain, and he didn't weep when Lee surrendered, he simply sank to the ground in exhaustion, too hungry and too weary to go on. He tried not to think of the war anymore; it was a long time ago and that kind of killing didn't really count. To his great regret he had killed one last time, and he was still paying for that mistake.

Inside was one of the prettiest women he'd ever laid eyes on, even with the scratches and torn clothes and sunburned skin. Her being pretty wasn't all of it, though. It was the way she felt in his arms when he'd carried her those last hundred yards to safety. Thinking about what she'd been through left him speechless and nearly sick to his stomach. He was afraid of what he'd do to any man who would commit such an act.

Just now in there, something behind her eyes told him that whatever had happened to her—and it must have been horrible—she was above it all. Better than anyone; proud, tough. She'd slug it out and get up again, ready to fight, in spite of her fear. He sensed, though, that she was also someone he should definitely steer clear of, for while he admired such courage, he could tell she came from a high-toned family. He sure didn't measure up to be worthy of her attention.

He had no bed to call his own but that one he made beneath the freight wagon wherever he and Wiley happened to be. He found his women at the Golden Sun Saloon, in their own perfumy beds, and then he went back to sleep on a blanket on the hard ground. That's all the kind of man he would ever be, and that little gal in there would set her sights on better. Way better. Probably already had. Sure didn't hurt to admire, but he'd best do it at a distance—a far, far distance.

The way she looked at him, he figured his best bet was to steer clear. She might want to come out and play once she got over whatever had happened, and he wasn't up to such antics. He had a hunch that with a woman like her, playing was all it would be. He'd never gone in for such nonsense and he didn't intend to start now.

It was a long time before he fell asleep. The ground felt hard and lumpy as mountain boulders, his thoughts more disturbing than usual, his desires riding close to the surface so that they prickled his skin and made him ache. When Wiley Moss came out at dawn to relieve himself around back of the station, Ben rose stiffly and unwillingly.

He went to stand a few feet from the old driver and couldn't help but ask, "She okay?"

"Durn right. Tough little critter. Ain't up to walking no more for a while. Feet's all blistered up. I told her we'd take her to Virginia City, seeing as how that's where we're going, and her, too. Soon as you fix that blamed wheel, that is."

Ben gritted his teeth as he buttoned up the front of his pants. "Why'd you tell her that?"

Wiley jerked a quick look at him. "Well, boy, she cain't walk it. What's the matter with you?"

"Yeah, but she could stay here, get all rested up, and we could send someone out to get her. A woman, maybe, who could be of some…some use to her." He bit off the words, blurted, "She'd be okay here. Only be another day."

"I'm plumb amazed at you, Ben Poole. Something has surely addled your brain. Leave that young'un out here alone to the mercy of whomsoever might come along? After what she's been through? Suppose the men that did this to her was to be following, and they found her here all alone? You ought to be ashamed for even having such thoughts."

"Aw, hell," Ben muttered. "I didn't mean…It's just— Shoot, I think I'll get on that wagon wheel. We need to be getting out of here. Costing Bannon money, his freight wagon being laid up this way."

"Well, that's better. I'll go in and git breakfast for all three of us. I'll shout when it's ready."

"Don't bother, I'll work right through. I can eat when

we get to Virginia City." Ben purely hated to make that concession; he did enjoy his food.

Wiley stomped away, shaking his head and muttering under his breath. Ben paid him no mind. He would stay away from the girl, no matter what Wiley Moss thought. She made him nervous as an old tom throwed down in a pen full of cute little pussy-cats. He had this urge to cuddle her up in his arms, and he had a feeling she'd scratch and spit something awful if he did. What he'd do if she started purring he had no idea.

She came out the door while he was sitting spraddle-legged behind the wagon wheel tending to its woes, and he couldn't help but watch her a moment. She was barefooted and limped slowly. The morning sunlight made a halo around her hair that needed combing real bad, but was as dark and shiny as a slab of polished walnut lumber.

She made her way carefully around the side of the station, and he blushed hotly, aware that she was headed for the privy.

"Think about the wheel, fool," he said, and went back to work self-consciously. Still, he couldn't help but watch her when she returned.

He could tell right away that while she might be bent, she wasn't broken. She held that head high and her shoulders struggled to square off even as she favored one leg. Whoever had done that to her ought to burn in hell for an eternity. He despised bullies who picked on the small and helpless. And men hurting women or children was his particular worst peeve.

He tapped at the metal, tapped again. The rim waddled, loose as a goose.

"I wanted to thank you," she said right behind him, and he squawked with surprise. "And tell you that breakfast is ready. I'm so hungry I could eat a whole bear if you'd go get me one. I have to say you look as if you could, too. But I can't feel right about sitting down to eat with you out here

working. So won't you please come in and join us before I
starve to death?"

He knew all along she'd talk like that. Light and airy and
sure of herself, babbling on and on like all he had to do was
pay attention. That cultured high-bred tone she'd had to learn
in some fancy back East school. He cleared his throat. It wasn't
polite to just plain not answer her question, and he guessed he
could sit here forever and she'd just stand there looking down
at him, waiting for a reply. It made the top of his head burn.

"No time. Besides, I'm not hungry. And even if I was, I
don't like Wiley's cooking." It was more than he'd meant to say.

Dessa studied the shoulder blades, drawn up as if to ward
off a blow. "Come on, Mr. Ben Poole. You wouldn't want to be
responsible for me falling down starved, would you?"

Her lips and tongue around his name, said like that, did
all sorts of strange things to him. One was to make him thump
his finger with the mallet.

Well, hell, if she put it that way.

He sucked on the mashed finger and scrabbled to his feet,
not daring to spare her a look as he strode to the house. He
forgot to hold the door for her and she swung it back open
and stood there glaring.

"I suppose you're mad at me about something I don't
remember doing," she said in a voice still hoarse from her
ordeal. "But that's no call for you to be rude, Ben Poole. You
act just like you were brought up in a barn."

He was fixing to seat himself in one of the chairs, but her
words caught him and he looked right at her. Her eyes were
flashing as bright as her hair did out in the sunlight, and he
could see his own reflection in the pupils. Instead of saying
anything, he just stared, right down into them, seeing her in
there. The real her, not the one she was putting on to cover her
feelings about what had happened.

"I apologize," he said softly, and pulled out a chair for her. "I'm sorry you were hurt, and I'm sorry I've acted like a fool. Sometimes I just plain don't know any better. Wiley says I ain't had proper raising."

He grinned crookedly, catching Dessa totally by surprise. Struck mute, she dragged her gaze away from him and gentled herself into the chair, babying the sore spots all over her battered body.

Wiley broke the long silence. "Might be you could tell us what happened out there. Who did that to you." He pointed at her with the tines of a fork.

She shuddered at the memory. She hurt all over, from the bottoms of her blistered feet to the top of her sunburned head. It could have been a lot worse and so she put off crying about it. For an instant she let her eyes drop to the plate and picked with trembling fingers at the edges of a tough biscuit. Ben was right about Wiley's cooking.

"Two men...well, one was just a boy. The other...he...he was horrid."

Remembering, she temporarily lost her voice and took a careful sip of the steaming black coffee. Placing the tin cup back on the table, she struggled to continue with her story.

Ben interrupted. "Ma'am, you don't have to do this now if you don't feel up to it. Plenty of time to tell the sheriff."

"No," she blurted. "I have to tell it. There's two dead men out there. They killed the stage driver and his...the man who rode with him on top."

Wiley brought a fist down on the slab table. "Aw, hell. Reckon who it was, Ben?"

The large blond man shook his head, furrows wrinkling the sun-gold skin across his forehead.

"Anyone else, ma'am?" Wiley asked.

"No, I was alone in the stage and they...they took me with them."

"Filthy skunks!" Wiley said.

Ben studied her a moment, the blue of his eyes frosty around the edges. "Did they...did they...hurt you?"

"Hurt me? Yes, Mr. Poole, they hurt me. But if you mean did they violate me, no, sir, they did not. They would have had to kill me to do so." She drew herself up and those green eyes shot sparks halfway across the room.

The change in her demeanor amazed Ben. The words were all brittle, angry, and defensive, as if he had accused her of something vile. He wondered how she had gotten out of the men's clutches, but decided not to ask. Not with the mood she was suddenly in. She'd probably throw her coffee at him.

For a while all three concentrated on the food on their plates without speaking further.

Wiley broke the silence. "Who you going to Virginia City to visit, ma'am?"

"What? Oh, my parents bought a mercantile store there, from a Mr. Yoes. Trevor and Mae Fallon. Do you know them?"

Ben stuffed a wad of biscuit in his mouth and shook his head, as if she had asked him, when all along she'd been addressing Wiley.

The old man sopped the hard biscuit in a pool of redeye gravy before replying. "No, but we ain't been back through long enough to meet anyone here lately. Ever one in that town finally gets their family belongings hauled in, we might get to rest a spell. Reed and Tressie Bannon's making a killing on this freight line."

Ben stopped chewing and appraised her with a blue-eyed gaze. "You gonna live in Virginia City?"

"No. Oh, no. We live in Kansas City. We were planning on getting the store going, hiring a manager, and then we're going to Denver for a few weeks. We fully intend to return home before winter."

Ben looked back down at his plate, at the strip of overcooked fatback. Wiley always did turn meat into leather before he considered it done.

Quickly Ben forgot the overdone meat and went back to considering the woman. She was rich and she wasn't going to be in town long. He considered that a good omen. Her presence disturbed the hell out of him, and he couldn't have explained it if he'd had to. Not even to Maggie or Rose, the only two women he'd ever been around, and both of whom he loved like the mother and sister he'd lost so long ago.

He couldn't even explain it to his friend Wiley Moss, and most especially not to himself.

He considered that the way he was feeling was probably what folks called smitten, and he wanted no part of it. It was god-awful uncomfortable. Fisting up the rest of his biscuit and the blackened strip of fatback, he kicked away from the table, making a terrible clatter.

"Got to get back on that wheel if we're ever going to be on our way. Nice to see you're okay this morning, ma'am, and I'm sure sorry about your ordeal. I expect Sheriff Moohn'll get up a posse first thing and put them boys on the end of a rope. And they'll want to send someone after the bodies before—" He broke off self-consciously. No sense talking about what a pack of wolves could do to dead men.

"My name is Dessa," she said, and favored him with the tiniest of smiles. Her lips were dry and cracked and the delicate skin on her face was scratched and burned; still, that was the most beautiful thing Ben Poole thought he'd ever seen in his life. That smile. Those eyes. That lovely name. Dessa.

He nearly fell over himself getting the hell out of there.

Wiley chuckled. "Like I say ever' chance I get, that boy ain't had much raising. You'll have to forgive him. Strange, though. I've known Ben a lot of years and that's the first time

I've ever seen him act so bumfoozled. Must be something in the air." He rolled light brown eyes up under wrinkled lids and chuckled again, then finished sopping the greasy gravy.

She eyed the unappetizing mess on her plate. She hadn't had a bite of decent food in a long while. Railroad fare was only a touch better than the poor meals the stage line furnished. Hunger pangs knotted her stomach. Hunger for civilized food like a light and fluffy omelette sprinkled with cheese, hemmed on the plate with thin slices of hickory- cured ham. She dearly hoped the town of Virginia City had a decent restaurant. More than that, she prayed for a hot bath and clean sheets and a soft featherbed mattress.

She sensed the older man watching her and glanced up. He dropped his gaze back to his plate, which was empty now. "Do you suppose I could clean up a bit before we leave?" she asked him.

"Oh, yes, ma'am. I'm purely sorry for not thinking. I'll draw you some water. There's a kettle on the stove. That'll take the chill off, and I'll clear out. You'll be alone here. They stopped having an agent here when the stages quit running but now and then. This place just kinda looks after itself when there ain't no one stopping over."

Moving like a cricket, the small man fetched a sweat-stained hat from a nail on the wall and crammed it on his head. "I'll just bring you that water, then leave you be. Sorry we ain't got nothing for you to put on."

She looked down at the filthy, tattered blue dress and shrugged. "I've got clothes in town. Mother and Father brought a trunk ahead for me so I could travel light. Those men, they dumped my satchel out all over the place, and stole my...stole my ring." She felt tears welling in her eyes and turned away to stare out the window. No sense being a baby. It was all over now, and she didn't want this kind man to think her weak.

Mitchell always said that inner strength was the only thing no one could take away from you. She wondered for the millionth time how someone had managed to kill him, with all that strength he had possessed.

Wiley opened the door, stopped, and turned back to her. "Don't you worry none. They'll get those varmints and string 'em up."

In a few moments he returned with a wooden bucket slopping over with water and set it on the table. "There's a wash pan over there on the stand. Sorry there's such mean supplies, but that rag'll have to do you."

She nodded and, as soon as he closed the door, began to undo the buttons of her dress. She was struck suddenly with a memory of wearing the teal-blue dress for the first time after picking it up from the dressmaker. Andrew had taken her to the park and they walked along the riverbank. A brisk wind caught at her hair, and he pushed a strand back away from her eyes and looked down at her. He loved her and she knew it, wondered why she couldn't return that love. It was as if she were looking for something in him that just wasn't there. A spark, an excitement of expectation, not knowing what tomorrow would bring. But he and Daddy had the future all worked out and in it was no room for the unexpected, the exciting. Andrew would continue to work for the Fallons and eventually, when Daddy retired, take over the business. With the only Fallon male heir dead, it would work out just fine, keep the business in the family.

Despite those plans, she spent the summer of this, her eighteenth year, searching through an assortment of men who satisfied her need for excitement, leaving Andrew dangling in the wings. Where he still dangled. This was the first time she'd thought of him since leaving Kansas City. What did love have to do with it?

She pulled the shredded dress gently down off one shoulder, then the other, wincing from her bruises. When she returned, she must tell Andrew that she wouldn't marry him, that she couldn't be the one he carried over the threshold into that exclusive house on the hill above the river. It would be hard. And hard on her parents, too. They already envisioned the grandchildren who would play beneath the large old oaks in their backyard. The small dark-haired boy who would fill the cold corners left in their hearts by Mitchell's death.

The ripped bodice and sleeves fell down around her waist, and she dipped the rag in the wash pan of cold water warmed with a splash from the black iron kettle on the stove. She had progressed to her legs, standing beside the chair with one foot propped up on it, when she glanced out the window to see Ben Poole driving the freight wagon around to the front of the station. Fascinated by his lithe movements as he wrapped the reins around the brake handle and hopped to the ground, she didn't realize that he was headed for the door until it was too late to do anything but gape at the sight of him.

As the door swung open, he looked right at her, dress hiked up above her thighs and one leg showing bare skin all the way to the swell of her buttocks.

Almost too late she remembered to cross her arms over her chest, but not before he glimpsed the rosy nipples and the sheen of creamy skin still moist from her bath. He expected her to turn away, but she didn't move an inch in any direction. Ben stood right where he was and got an eyeful. It was as if both had been temporarily but instantly frozen by a blizzard wind from high off the Montana mountains. They would simply remain that way, staring at each other, until sunlight could thaw them.

She licked her lips, and hugged herself tighter. Something strange was going on all over her body, and it wasn't the aches and pains from her ordeal, either. It was a wet and warm sensation that turned cold, then hot as it rushed through her vitals.

He wanted to make a clever remark and set them both at ease. But he never had been good at that, and so he settled for saying nothing at all and enjoying the sights. Her legs were longhand shapely, the skin creamy except where great long scratches and ugly bruises marred their beauty. The inside of one thigh sported a brutish purple mark almost the size of his fist, and he was filled with a need to bash in somebody's head for hurting her like that. Fool that he was, he didn't look at the exposed breasts before she crossed her arms protectively across her chest. Maggie would have thought nothing of such a thing. This one would. She continued to watch him like a stricken animal in the woods.

He had a sudden all-over feeling of what love would be like with her. The prospect both thrilled and frightened him. What would be expected of a man who loved such a gorgeous woman? More, he'd allow, than he could give. He had to move from the spot to which he was staked; somehow he had to simply back out the door and close it. He tried to shift his feet, but nothing happened. God, she was lovely.

"Ben Poole, what the thunderation you think you're doing?" Wiley Moss shouted, and, coming up behind him, whopped at his backside with his hat.

"Quit peering in at the young'un. You got no manners at all, boy? Get your tail outta there 'fore I thrash you."

The spell broken, Dessa laughed at the sight of the wiry little man flailing away at the much larger Ben Poole, who had turned a vivid red and was making tracks as fast as he could, impeded as he was by Wiley's hat swatting around on him.

On thinking about the incident, she wondered what in the world had come over her, letting Ben see her like that and enjoying his reaction as well as her own. This might call for a little looking into. Getting better acquainted with Ben Poole could liven up the two or three weeks she would be forced to spend in the godforsaken town of Virginia City out here at the ends of the earth. Again, she wondered why in the world her father had chosen to open a mercantile in a town mined out and bypassed by the railroad.

Soon her mind was occupied with seeing her parents and she put memories of the brief but explosive encounter with Ben in the back of her mind. Sore and achy as her body was, it took all her concentration to endure the rough ride aboard the freight wagon.

The three arrived in Virginia City around mid-afternoon. Dessa was weak with exhaustion and hunger. She could hardly wait to find her way to her parents' quarters above the mercantile, get out of the torn and soiled clothes, and luxuriate in a hot bath. She thought of the food she would order afterward when they went out to dinner. Perhaps a thick steak and baked potato, some vegetables if they had any out here in the wilderness.

Ben had scarcely spoken during the trip, but Wiley had kept up a running commentary on subjects all the way from wondering who had been killed in the stage robbery to how good it would be to get off that blamed wagon for an hour or two.

He drove directly to the freight depot and pulled up. "Big Ben here can see you safely to your hearth's door, child," he told Dessa, then aimed a hard stare at his friend. "And you keep your eyes and hands where they belong, young sir. This is a lady."

Ben flushed. "You don't have to tell me that, I know. You take her. I'll deal with Bannon."

"And have some yahoo make light of her? With you along, they'll think twice. Now do as I say. Take this little girl home so she can rest. I'll get this done and go talk to Sheriff Moohn about the killing."

With that, Wiley leaped from the wagon and headed for the depot door.

"He takes no lip from anyone," Ben said.

"If you want away from me so badly, I'll just get down and walk," she said, and started to rise from the seat.

Her tone surprised him. What had he done? "I'll take you." He took up the reins and clucked at the horses, the movement throwing her back onto the seat.

On the verge of collapse, she hung on dearly and snapped, "Don't put yourself out. You know, Mr. Moss is right about you. You're plain rude. Not having any upbringing is no excuse. Or maybe everyone here in the territories is shy of any manners."

Ben colored. "I've got plenty of manners. You ought'n to act so uppity about being from the States. It ain't no big deal, little Miss Fancy Pants."

Dessa blew a strand of hair from her face. "Well, Kansas City is certainly a bigger deal than this…this rat hole. It's unsanitary and the people look like bums. I can see now why you act like you do, living in such squalor."

In his anger Ben smacked the rumps of the horses with the fat reins. "You act that way around folks in town, and you won't have any friends. They'll stay away from you like the plague."

She swung around and glared. "Well, maybe I don't want any friends here. Anyway, we won't be—" She broke off when Ben reined in the horses and rose to his feet, a look of dismay on his handsome face.

"Lord God almighty," he breathed.

What was left of Yoes Mercantile smoldered thin tendrils of smoke that blew away in the wind.

"What? What is it?"

"Did you say Yoes Mercantile? Your folks bought Yoes Mercantile?"

She nodded dumbly and stared at the blackened heap of rubbish. "Was that…?"

Ben badly wanted to turn right around and head the

other way, but it was too late. He had driven her right up to the blackened ruins that had once been a fine two-story structure. He wanted to gather her in his arms when she cried out forlornly, but he didn't get a chance.

She scrambled down from the seat, swayed on her feet, moaned. "Mother, Daddy. Where are they? What happened? Oh, look. What am I going to do? We've got to find them."

The sad desperation in her voice tore at his heart, and he did what he had wanted to do a moment earlier. He hopped from the wagon and simply folded her up in both arms. He held her trembling body, shielded her against his chest, and did his best to protect her from the onslaught of emotions.

She leaned limply into the embrace, and soon her tears moistened the front of his shirt. He put his lips in the tangle of her dark hair and closed his eyes. Poor little thing. What would happen to her next?

Three

For a long while Dessa remained in Ben's arms.

She tried not to think of what was yet to come. If she never asked, would she have to find out what had happened to her parents? If she remained hidden within his strength, then she wouldn't have to face the truth. He was hard and soft at the same time, and power emanated from him like warmth from a fire. A gentle power that didn't frighten her. For the moment it was enough to ease the dread of what was yet to come.

Filled with hopeful denial, she sniffed into his chest, sniffed again, and stopped crying.

He took her by the upper arms and pushed her away to look into her face. "You okay?"

She nodded woodenly.

"Okay, then. We'll find out what happened. The sheriff will know. And then we'll…well, we'll do what has to be done."

"Yes, fine. That's what we'll do," she said in a voice as flat as a wooden plank.

He studied the glazed look that had clouded the shine of her green eyes. "You're sure you're okay. You're not going to faint or anything."

"I don't faint. Let's find the sheriff."

Without his help she scrambled up onto the wagon seat. After climbing aboard, Ben smacked the horse's rumps with the heavy leather reins and turned the wagon in the street, heading back toward the sheriff's office. Dessa clung to the edges of the seat, feeling as if her world had spiraled completely out of control. How could so much go wrong in so short a time? It was like a nightmare that had begun with the stage robbery and hadn't yet ended. She felt as if she had fallen into a void that had no bottom or anything to cling to.

She glanced at her companion. He sat tall, head and shoulders held stiffly, facing straight ahead with a somber expression tightening the finely sculpted features. Sweat gleamed along the line of his jaw and a small muscle danced just beneath his ear. She felt desolate, but at the same time sheltered by this stoic giant.

"Ben Poole," she said softly.

He glanced at her.

"I'm glad you're with me. Thank you."

"Yes, well…fine." He didn't know what to say, and so just left it at that. His heart ached for her. He understood what she was going through, for he had never forgotten the day bushwhackers had murdered his entire family, left them strewn like butchered animals for him to find when he returned to the ransacked cabin. A boy only just thirteen.

Oh, God, yes, he knew, and he felt her loss keenly.

At the sheriff's office Ben helped Dessa off the wagon seat. She stumbled and he clasped her arm, guiding her through the open door. He feared she would fall, but some inner strength held her upright. He had a very bad feeling about this.

Sheriff Walter Moohn reclined in his chair, boots propped on the bottom drawer of a mammoth oak desk. He picked at his teeth with a broom straw and made no comment until the two young people were inside with the door shut.

Then he said, "Seen you come into town, wondered where you got your passenger. Old Wiley ain't been by yet, expect him soon for our usual game of checkers. This little gal looks tuckered. Set her down, Ben. What's up?"

Dessa wobbled but didn't take the empty chair. "The store that burned—where are my folks? Are they okay?"

Moohn sat up, boot soles hitting the floor with a thud. "Mr. and Mrs. Fallon, wasn't it? Bought the Yoes Mercantile. It burnt last night, still smoldering, I reckon. Nothing we could do. I'm sorry, girl, plumb sorry. You got kin you can wire, someone who can come help you take care of…uh, the arrangements?"

"Arrangements?" Dessa swayed, reached out, and Ben took her hand. "No. No, not my parents. But they just got here. How could this happen, Ben?" She cast a pleading glance up into his concerned face. Make it go away, she pleaded silently. Tell the sheriff he's wrong, that he's talking about someone else, not Mother and Daddy. But no one said anything.

Ben's eyes gleamed and he blinked several times, quickly. He wanted to say something, anything that would ease her sorrow, but no words came.

She swallowed hard, asked in a whisper what she already knew. "Are they dead?" This was crazy. It couldn't be happening. She wanted to wail and pound her chest like women of old. Instead she just stood there, vision all but blank to anything but memories.

In the narrow tunnel of sight she watched the sheriff nod sadly, felt her knees buckle, and sank into a vast, deep cavern.

Ben caught her before she hit the floor, lifting her in his arms like he'd done only the night before when she'd come stumbling toward the stage station like someone half dead.

"Damn it, Moohn, couldn't you have been easier on her?" His voice caught over the words.

The gruff sheriff shrugged. "Sorry, boy. I don't know no way to tell someone their folks is dead but to say it right out.

It's a sad and sorry thing, but it happens. And I have to deal with it best I can.

"Why'n't you get her a place to stay. The bodies'll keep till she comes out of it. Now go on."

Ben moved through the door and stood on the boardwalk outside the sheriff's office, momentarily at a loss. People stepped around him while they eyed the unconscious girl in his arms. He thought about the stagecoach holdup. He should have told the sheriff. Then he looked down into the pale face of the girl. A bruise highlighted one cheek and several scratches ran down the side of her neck. Anger rose once again from deep in his throat. He'd see those bastards strung up before this was over. Meanwhile, Wiley would have to take care of telling Moohn about the robbery. He had himself a big enough problem right here, and he wasn't sure what to do with her. No money meant no hotel room.

That left only one place for Ben to take Dessa, and that was the Golden Sun Saloon and Rose Langue, whose penchant for caring for the lost and orphaned had once saved Ben himself. Rose and Maggie would know what to do with his sorely wounded girl. He stepped down into the dusty street and strode through meandering horses, wagons, and people, carrying Dessa as easily as he would have a stack of down pillows. He nodded grimly at those who watched, but offered no explanation.

Dessa awoke to a still and mellow darkness. Across the strange room in which she lay, a candle sputtered, sending out a frail beacon but doing little to illuminate her surroundings. She lay up to her ears in a feather mattress, and no longer wore her ragged clothes. Instead she was wrapped in a soft gown, its fabric soothing and fragrant. As she grew more aware, she heard distant music and the peal of occasional feminine laughter broken by rougher guffaws, obviously male in origin.

She turned her head and moaned. The back of her neck ached and there was a throbbing at her temples. She licked at lips so dry her tongue stuck to them. In the gloom she made out a pitcher on the side table and near it a glass. She raised herself on one elbow, feeling every muscle in her body cry out, and filled the glass with water. For a few blessed moments she remembered nothing, as if her head were full of cotton wool and nothing else, as if all memory hung beyond some darkened curtain waiting for her to pull it open. All she knew was the cool sweetness of the water and the softness of the bed and the soreness of her body. A stranger's body cradling a stranger's mind.

When memory of what had happened came back to her, it came suddenly and brutally, all in a rush, making her cry out. The robbery, the escape from the two awful outlaws, Ben Poole and Wiley Moss taking care of her, the sheriff's dreadful words.

How could this be? How could she go on? It wasn't fair. She'd struggled so hard to stay alive and return to her parents, and now they had died. How could they do that? Her heart and soul ached; her brain felt numb. No answers came.

She finished the glass of water and lay back in the bed. A welcome darkness enveloped her once again.

Seated at a table with Rose, Ben finished his sorry tale of Dessa Fallon's troubles and the cold-blooded killing of the stage driver and the man riding shotgun. He sensed her gaze waver and glanced up to see shrewd eyes studying him intently.

"What is it?"

Rose blinked and looked down at the table, then quickly back up into his face. "My darling Ben, you're worse than this old gal when it comes to being a pushover for a sad story."

"Yeah," he said, and grinned a bit. "And where do you suppose I got it from, dear Rose?"

Rose shook her head, loosening a curl from the blond mass of piled-high tresses. "Don't lay that at my feet. I just nourished me a starving pup, and look what I got. A great big galoot a touch too soft for his own good. You can't even put two bits together, Ben. And why is that?"

"Aw, hell, Rose. You know. Maggie always needs something, and then there's Sarah and her twins. Their daddy getting killed like he did, and leaving them and their ma with nothing."

Rose laid her hand over his fingers, which nervously picked at the rough wooden surface. "Wasn't your fault, Ben. When are you going to realize a wild bullet is just that? You were doing what needed done and he got in the way."

He shook his head. "I should have taken more care, Rose. A man has to be responsible for his actions, and that's all there is to that. Killing a man, Rose, that's just about the worst thing that can happen. I was sick of it when I got here, so sick I wanted to die."

Rose got up from her chair. "I'll go up and look in on your poor little orphan, Ben. You have yourself another brew and turn in. Go crawl under that blamed wagon and sleep on the hard ground one more night. Maybe one day you'll get tired of punishing yourself for all the ills of the world."

Ben grinned up at her. "Aw, hell, Rose. I'm doing just fine. Between you and Maggie babying and mothering me, I reckon I'll make out. I think I'll pass on the beer and get me some sleep. I'll check back on Dessa in the morning before me and Wiley leave out."

Rose watched Ben saunter through the batwing doors and out into the night.

If it hadn't been for Ben, she would have gone crazy in those years after Jarrad Lincolnshire fetched his wife and put her out there on the hill in that castle he'd built. And turned his back on Rose like their love had never been. She would never love another man, but being occupied with Ben Poole when he rode in, scarred and half dead from the war, had saved her sanity. He had become like a son to her. And now she could walk right out in the middle of the street and stare up at that pretentious stone monster clinging to the side of the mountain and feel nothing. Well, almost nothing. The Englishman had died last year, his wife and children returned to England, and the castle stood empty, as did the ugly, washed-out mine above the town.

Rose shrugged and tossed off the memories. Best let the past remain just that. Dead and gone and buried. She lifted the skirts of her shiny gold dress and went up the stairs to see about her newest charge.

The next time Dessa awoke, it was to brilliant sunshine. The red brocade drapes had been drawn aside to let in the morning, and before memory claimed her once again, she actually felt a lift in spirits. What a lovely room, with its bright reds and shades of rich cream. She lay nestled within thick layers of silk and satin. Who lived in such glorious splendor? And how had she gotten here?

The flood of bitter memories came then and she began to cry. So intense was her grief over the death of her parents that she didn't immediately recall the ride into town with Ben Poole or the visit to the sheriff's office. When she finally did, she wiped her eyes and crawled from the bed, wincing with the pain in her sore feet.

On the other side of the room stood something she had never thought to see out here on the frontier. It was a bathtub! In all its glorious splendor. What a marvelous place. Where was she? Had Ben Poole brought her here, undressed her?

She crept to the door, opened it a crack, and listened. Deathly silence greeted her and she stuck her head out to look around. Other doors besides this one opened off one side of a wide balcony. Quietly she eased over to the rail. Down below she saw a great mahogany bar backed by oval mirrors and paintings. A glorious Cremona rested against one wall. She had heard piano music. How many nights she had danced the hours away in the arms of one beau or another, a player piano such as that tinkling gaily in the background. She'd not thought to see one out here on the frontier.

She wiped tears from her eyes at memories of that life when Mother and Daddy were alive.

From below came a sound and she looked to see a bearded gentleman wearing a striped shirt, black pants, and an apron. He hummed softly and mopped at the plank floor among tables with chairs turned upside down on their tops. No one else was in sight and no sounds came from behind the row of closed doors along the veranda. Hadn't she heard music, laughter? Or had that been in the night? She shook her head, confused.

Dessa went back in the room where she had awakened. She didn't know what to do. There was no sign of her clothing and she considered it rude to open any one of the armoires in the large room. She was stuck there in a nightgown, and beginning to need to relieve herself.

A male voice boomed out below and floated upward. After a moment someone tapped on the door. She crossed both arms over her breasts, stood there at a loss for a couple of seconds, then bounded back into the bed and under the covers as the door swung open, accompanied by a greeting.

"You awake, ma'am? It's me. Ben Poole. You okay?" All this he said before he caught sight of her, bedclothes wadded up under her chin and eyes wide with dismay.

"Where am I?" she asked, then thought what a foolish greeting for this man who had obviously taken such care of her.

He stopped in the center of the room. "I didn't mean to bother you. I just wanted to see if you were..." He glanced around and flushed. "Wiley...Wiley and me...we're just leaving out. Wanted to see if you need anything."

"Clothes," Dessa said in a small voice. "I don't have any clothes." Her eyes filled with tears that she couldn't control, tears that had nothing to do with an absence of clothing.

"Aw, honey, don't cry," Ben said, and came to her like a great bear, kneeling on the floor beside the bed and gathering her in his arms. He patted awkwardly at her head, then said softly against her cheek, "Go ahead and cry. That's a girl. Cry and get it over with. It's okay. I'm sorry about your ma, and pa, I wish it could have been some other way, but it'll be all right, I promise. It'll finally be all right."

She fisted up wads of his rough homespun shirt and clung tightly while she grieved. This had to stop. She had to get hold of herself. So much had happened so fast that her normally tough exterior had been badly damaged.

"I don't usually do this," she snuffled into his chest.

And I don't usually do this, Ben thought, but didn't say. Holding her in his arms produced a rush of all kinds of feelings he just wasn't up to dealing with. An occasional romp with one of Rose's girls never produced such enormous compassion, such heart-rending, head-pounding need. Not of a physical nature, but simply the desire to take away Dessa's pain, to make her laugh again. To have her smile at him and care about him and...

Holding her got to be too much. He grasped both her wrists and put her away from him, firmly but gently. She had stopped the harsh sobbing, but tears still leaked from the corners of her eyes when he released her. He dared not touch her again, not the way he was reacting to being near her.

He rose. "You gonna be okay now?"

'Yes, thank you."

"Well, then, I'd better...go on. Maggie'll be here in a while and she'll get you something to wear. Your dress... it was just ruined."

Dessa darted a quick look up into his face. Had he helped

undress her? Seen her naked? A fire burst into flame between her breasts and spread up her throat.

But when she started to challenge him, she found he had left, the sound of his boots silenced by the rug. Crawling from the bed, she hurried across the room and out onto the balcony in time to see him fetch a disreputable hat off a hook on the wall beside the door below, cram it down on his head, and burst outside like he was pursued by the devil himself.

From down the hallway a small brunette came out of one of the rooms. She was dressed only in a scandalous red corset and filmy black robe. Mesmerized, Dessa remained at the railing, clutching it with the fingers of one hand and watching the woman approach.

She smiled at Dessa and the tired eyes lit up. "Hi. You must be Ben's friend. I'm Maggie, Ben's friend also. How are you this morning?"

Her voice was low, and when she spoke, she unconsciously moved her exquisite hands as if using them to accent the meaning of her words.

"I don't have any clothes," Dessa said again, as if that would explain her standing out in the open in her blistered bare feet and clad only in a nightgown.

Maggie eyed Dessa's lean, athletic frame and shook her head. Tapping scarlet-nailed fingers to her lips, she considered the problem in silence. At last she reached a decision. "Virgie's built some like you. We'll get you something to do you for now."

Maggie trotted off, leaving Dessa to stare after her. She considered her surroundings for a moment or two, leaned over the railing, and looked down once more.

All of a sudden she put everything together and realized what kind of a place this was. Ben Poole had brought her to a brothel. That big grinning heathen had dumped her in with a bunch of...a bunch of fancy women. The little trollop called Maggie was no doubt much more than just a friend of Ben's. And what did Ben Poole think, bringing her to a place like this?

She stormed back into the room, stood in the middle, and glared around. Now it was easy to see what this room, that luxuriously appointed bed, was used for.

The door burst open and she whirled to face whomever might enter. "I have to get out of here. Now. I can't stay here in this...this disgusting place. Get my clothes. I'll wear my own clothes, not some whore's."

"Whoa, now, child," the regal woman with a head full of blond curls said. "Calm down. You've had a tough time, but don't you go getting snippy with me. This 'disgusting' place, as you call it, sheltered you when you had nowhere else to go. And I'll not have you looking down your pretty little nose at me or my girls.

"Now, if you want to cry over your troubles or throw things, that's fine, but you just settle yourself down when it comes to insulting me."

Under the tirade Dessa staggered backward a step or two. She was used to getting her own way. This didn't bode well, this beautiful blond woman who was obviously the head madam of this whorehouse, talking to her like she was one of her soiled girls.

She drew herself up, ready to fight, fists clenched at her sides and mouth set firmly.

"That's better. Look me right in the eye, child. Stand up to me. But don't you dare act better than me, because you're not. And you're not better than my girls. One more step in the way you're going and you might not have many choices, either. It can happen that fast. If it weren't for Ben Poole and a few others, you'd have slept on the street last night, and who knows what would have happened to you there."

Dessa nodded. The woman was right, and she felt

chagrined. Her daddy would have been ashamed of her behavior. She raised her chin and refused to let the tears begin again. There was too much to do for any more crying.

The older woman crossed the room and put an arm around her. She smelled of sweet talcum and lavender, and wore a sunyellow dress with a massive skirt and a hat tilted perkily on her carefully coiffed curls. She carried a folded parasol over one arm and her reticule over the other. These she placed on a padded chaise near the bathtub.

"Now, child, if you can see fit to speak, perhaps we can visit a spell, get acquainted while Maggie fetches you some decent clothing." She grinned wryly. "My name is Rose Langue, and this is my place of business."

Dessa nodded and sank to the edge of the bed. Her feet still bothered her and the muscles in the backs of her legs ached from the long trek. But nothing hurt quite so badly as her heart, and it was breaking. "I'm sorry," she said, lower lip trembling.

"And I, too, dear. About your parents, that is. What a terrible loss. But we mustn't dwell on it overmuch. You've got to look forward. Do you have any people?"

"No. Just my parents…and me. My brother Mitchell died in the war, and there is no one else. I don't know what to do." She nearly cried the words, but controlled her emotions so that she didn't act like a baby.

"There, there. Take a deep breath. What about money? Your parents owned the mercantile that burned. Did they have anything else? Any other property, any funds?"

"Oh, yes. My father owns—I mean owned— general stores all over the country. Besides several in Kansas City, he had two in St. Louis and three in Denver. And since the Union Pacific laid out their route to Promontory, he'd had a few more built. I'm not sure how many. Everyone wondered why in the world he bought one here, and I guess we'll never know now."

"Well, then, there shouldn't be a problem. You'll need to send a wire to whoever helped your father run his business. There are surely accountants, attorneys, and the like who will need to be notified, if the sheriff hasn't done so already. They will no doubt send you some money and you can go back home."

Dessa stared down at her hands lying limply in her lap. Go home? Ride that dreadful stage and that noisy, gritty train all the way back to Kansas City, when she had just suffered such a horrific time getting here? Well, she simply couldn't think of that.

"I can't go home. Not yet. Not after what's happened. I don't think I could bring myself to climb back on board that dreadful stage."

Rose chuckled. "I can't say as I blame you for that. Riding very far in one of those contraptions will shake your guts right out."

Dessa gasped. She wasn't used to ladies talking in such a bold manner. But then she supposed women who could live on this frontier had to learn to give up some niceties in order to survive. Delicate speech probably was the first to go, right along with modesty, if her own experience was any example.

Rose studied her a moment, then sat beside her on the bed and took her hand. "Ben told me what happened. You were very brave and very lucky. Traveling alone, a girl like you can get in all kinds of trouble. It seems strange that your parents would allow such a thing. But you're here now, and safe. And you'll get through this, strong child that you are. We'll help you, and so will Ben."

Dessa clenched her fingers together in her lap. She wanted to defend her parents, tell Rose all about the gentleman escort, employee of her father's company, entrusted with her safekeeping. And how he'd been lured away by a weakness for gambling and loose women. Lured to a place much like this.

Four

While Dessa and Rose ate breakfast at the Continental House, a large band of men rode out of town accompanied by a ballyhoo of shouts and shrill whistles.

"Walter and his posse," Rose remarked, and nibbled at a puffy biscuit.

"After the men who—" Dessa broke off. The china teacup rattled from her fingers into its saucer.

"Yes. Too much of that going on around here lately. Right after the war there was a spurt of outlawry, but things were cooling down with the failure of the mines. Got to where there wasn't much to steal. And old Sheriff Plummer getting himself hanged as the head of a pack of road agents put a damper on thievery for a while. But that was a few years back, and now, I don't know. I just don't know." She lowered her head to fork eggs into her mouth, then went on. "They say there's a passel of road agents hiding out in these mountains. Some even claim that devil Yank to be leading them. Say he come out of the Union Army crazy in the head and out to avenge ever' shot fired at him. I don't know about that. You'd think they'd move on down South and start robbing the trains, what with all that excitement down in Promontory last year. Imagine riding coast to coast by rail.

"I suppose, though, it's a little harder to rob a train than it is a stagecoach or bank. Won't be long before they'll figure it out, I expect."

In Dessa's mind the only questions she could really consider were those regarding the death of her parents, so she added nothing to the conversation. Even the brief hours spent with that awful man Coody and his partner had blurred with the reality of her tragic loss. .

Rose glanced up and patted her perfectly painted red lips with a linen napkin. "What is it, child? You've scarcely touched your food. Eat, keep up your strength. You'll need it."

Rose's no-nonsense approach lent Dessa a bit of courage. Whorehouse madam or no, she acted like she really cared—and her not even knowing Dessa or her troubles till yesterday. It was hard to keep from crying if she let herself dwell on what had happened, so she bravely lifted the fork and delicately deposited a minuscule bit of potato on her tongue.

Rose shook her head. She saw the tears pooling in the child's eyes and didn't want to chastise her, but just the same, if she'd eat more, she'd feel better.

"I don't know what to do, Rose," Dessa said, and lay down the fork. It was no use; she couldn't swallow another bite. She might as well have been trying to eat a chunk out of the boardwalk out front.

"Oh, I know you don't. But one thing at a time, without thinking ahead, is the best course for now. I spoke to Walter, and he knew nothing about who to notify, so I suppose you should start there."

Dessa nodded. "There's just our attorney, the accountant, people who helped run the business. I suppose I should send a wire."

"Then we'll go to the telegraph office from here."

Being completely alone was a terrible feeling, and she welcomed Rose's kindness. All she wanted was to coil up in a dark corner until everything righted itself. An orphan at eighteen. What an awful thing.

"I'm so grateful to you. There's no one else. No one. If my parents had any relations, I don't know about them. They married back in Pennsylvania and moved to Kansas City. I understand that my grandfather was in the same business as my father and set him up on his first venture. But he died when I was small. There were no other children. My grandmother died before I was born."

"My mother never spoke of her family. I always had the feeling they didn't approve of the marriage and so wanted nothing to do with us. I think they lived in Virginia somewhere, but I'm not sure. My father said once that Mother left home with only the clothes on her back, running away to marry him. I don't even know the family name."

Dessa picked up the linen napkin and wiped at her fingertips, then glanced across the table at Rose. "So you see, I'm quite alone, and I'll just have to manage on my own. What I don't know is whether I should have them buried here or take them back to…back to Kansas City."

Rose studied the charcoal circles under the girl's green eyes. She couldn't imagine her turning around and making that dreadful trip by coach and train, and worse, taking along with her two charred lumps of human flesh that once were her beloved parents.

"Oh, child. What do you think of this? We'll have two lovely wooden caskets constructed. Mason Yell is a fine craftsman, and can do just what you want. Then we'll find a peaceful spot out at Boot Hill—I'll go with you, if you like—and just let the Reverend Blair speak a nice service. Everyone in town will come, give your parents a proper send-off. They would approve, I'm sure."

"No parent would want to see their child suffer any more than she must over this. I can assure you of that. Your mother would want what is the simplest for you to manage."

The pooling tears spilled over and ran down Dessa's cheeks, but she made no sound at all. This was all too much, and if it weren't for this brothel madam, she had no idea what she would do. What her friends back in Kansas City would think of that, she had absolutely no idea. Imagine that, imagine that indeed.

She patted at the tears and nodded.

"Fine, then that's settled. You can stay with me awhile until you decide what you want to do. And do me a favor, will you?"

Dessa nodded again.

"Be nice to Ben Poole. He's walking on his own tongue dogging your every step." Rose smiled brightly, and though it looked somewhat forced, it made Dessa feel a bit better.

"I haven't been anything but nice to him. He's just so… well, so different from any man I've ever met."

Rose chuckled. "Well, I wouldn't have used the word different—it's too bland. Ben has his own row to hoe, and so far he's doing a damn fine job of it, seeing how he started. A half-starved young pup, dodging every time a gun went off, haunts of the war in those startling eyes of his. We all thought for a while he was a raving lunatic, but it turned out he was just a frightened boy. When he came here, he couldn't even read. My Maggie taught him. Maggie was abandoned by her parents, who were traveling to Utah with the Mormon train. Both being orphans, in a way, they just took up with each other, formed a sort of family. She's a smart little thing and doing her best, too.

"You know, child. You'd do well to consider what folks have had to put up with before you go judging what they've done with their lives."

Dessa hung her head. While she was happy that the subject had veered away from the funeral and her parents' death, she wasn't sure she liked this tack, either.

"I haven't judged anyone." Even as she said it, Dessa knew the words weren't exactly true.

"It's all right. Don't get upset, it was just a reminder that we can't be too harsh till we know all the rocks scattered in other folks' paths.'"

After wiring Kansas City, Rose sent Dessa back to rest in her room at the Golden Sun and went to arrange for the caskets. Seeing no reason for delay, Dessa decided to schedule the funeral for the next day. Rose had Ed at the Post print a simple announcement about the services and hired Dickey Slater to tack them up around town. She assured Dessa that everyone who could possibly get away would be at Boot Hill the next day for the funeral.

Dessa thought how odd it was that total strangers would be seeing her parents off on their final journey.

All afternoon she dealt with wires of sympathy from the Fallons' many friends in Kansas City. A steady stream was delivered to the Golden Sun, carried by barefoot boys proud of being charged with the duty. Dessa noticed that Rose always pressed a shiny coin in each boy's palm before shooing him on his way.

Late that day a wire came from the Cluney & Brown law firm with a transfer note for the bank in Virginia City. Dessa was no longer broke. She might be homeless, but she now had a bank account.

The only thing she could think of buying was a black dress for the funeral. At the dressmaker's she posed rigidly while the plump woman took her measurements and then fitted a cloth pattern to her body.

The woman had a strange way of conversing past a mouthful of pins. Dessa supposed that after a time one might grow to understand the mumbled words, but she simply nodded politely and occasionally murmured a noncommittal reply.

Once freed of the pieces of fabric, she donned the dress loaned to her by the girl they called Virgie. She felt extremely conspicuous. Its low-cut lace bodice revealed much too much of her bosom. She had borrowed a little jacket from Rose that helped some, and slipped into it as Mrs. Fabrini emptied her mouth of pins.

"I'll put this together tonight. Come for a fitting first thing in the morning and don't worry. It will be ready for the funeral. I am very fast. Ask anyone, they will tell you. Mrs. Fabrini is very fast." She stuck out her right hand, palm up to reveal the pads of her fingers. "See, see how hard they are. That comes from pushing the needle. Pushing and pushing it, day and night. Why I ever got into this, I don't know. But everyone needs dresses, yes? Cooking was my only other choice, and the Lord knows that would be my downfall."

Mrs. Fabrini pounded at her ample stomach with both hands. "This is what I get for cooking for Mr. Fabrini. Imagine if I cooked for everyone in this town all day, every day. No, it's better I sew the dresses." She lifted her shoulders in a shrug. "Still, I never get the new dress myself. There is never time, what with everyone else needing one for a funeral or a wedding or whatever. You come here from where, child?"

The conversation that had flowed from the woman once she unpinned her lips amazed Dessa. She managed to answer the question. It set the woman off and running once again.

"Ah, yes, that place. We were through there, Mr. Fabrini and I. Coming out West to make our fortune in the gold mines." A great booming laugh shook the homely woman. "It is a great and nasty town, is it not? But not nearly so stinking as New York. When we got off the ship, I told Mr. Fabrini that if we had to remain in that place, I would probably just kill both of us and put us out of our misery. And so, him not wanting me to do that, we started west. What a trip, what a trip. I am telling no one just how horrible it really was, because they would not be believing me.

Mrs. Fabrini patted at Dessa's arm and shoved her toward the door. 'You must leave now, child, or I will not get a thing done but talking your leg off."

Out on the walk, Dessa leaned back against the building and laughed. She couldn't help it, the conversation had been so wonderfully distracting. Enthralled by Mrs. Fabrini's tale, she had been able to forget for a brief interlude that she had gone to the dressmaker for something to wear to her parents' funeral.

Wiley and Ben rode back into Virginia City at dusk, and Ben gladly left Wiley to his beloved paperwork and nightly checker game with Walter Moohn. He told himself he was going to the Golden Sun for his usual glass of brew before hunting up some supper, but the moment he stepped inside and glanced around, he felt disappointed. It had nothing to do with wetting his whistle, either. He didn't see Dessa Fallon anywhere, but why should he? A girl like her would not hang around in a hurdy-gurdy house. Rose had her hidden away upstairs, no doubt.

Maggie and two or three of the regular girls were dancing with their partners, but he didn't see Rose. He ordered the beer and glanced toward the stairway. Maggie snuck up behind him and touched his arm, making him slosh foam over the rim of his glass.

"Want to dance?" she asked with a hint of the devil flashing in her hazel eyes. She knew Ben refused to dance in public and liked to get at him about it.

"Buy you a beer instead?" he offered, but kept his eyes on the upstairs balcony.

"Okay. Who you looking for?" Maggie leaned an elbow on the bar and the motion revealed the fullness of her breasts spilling from the low-cut neckline.

Ben pulled his gaze up to her heart-shaped face. He loved her as if she were the sister he missed so much, but sometimes she could be annoying with her teasing. Just like that sister would be had she lived no doubt.

He grinned at her. "Rose. I'm looking for Rose."

"Sure, you big liar." Maggie sipped at the beer. "She's pretty, but kind of snobbish, don't you think?"

"Who, Rose?"

"Who, Rose? Oh, Ben, who do you think? That poor little thing you come striding in here with yesterday. Carrying her like she was some prize you'd won."

Ben remembered the soft touch of Dessa's breast against his arm, the suppleness of hip and thigh as he'd carried her across the street and into the Golden Sun. He thought of the silkiness of her hair tickling at his throat and her head tucked in against his shoulder, the bruise on the inside of her pale thigh when he'd shoved open the door and caught her bathing earlier that morning out at the stage stop. Quickly he gulped down the rest of the beer.

"Just wanted to make sure she's doing okay," he grumbled at Maggie, and stomped across the wooden floor, his worn boots thunking loud to show his annoyance.

"Where you going, Ben?" Maggie asked.

"Going to find me some supper, then off to bed."

"You coming back here for bed? Might get your mind and something else off that little thing who's much too fancy for the likes of you. If you'd like, I'll tell Virgie."

Ben glowered and Maggie ran back to the dance floor giggling.

A fellow in dusty pants and faded shirt handed her his token and hugged her frail body up close. Ben didn't see how she could put up with that all the time, but he tried to understand Maggie's life and why she had to live it the way she did. She might dance with anyone for a token, but Rose never made the girls take a man they didn't like to one of the cribs. That was strictly up to them. And Maggie was fussy that way. Very fussy indeed.

He hadn't been there with her since he was sixteen and Rose sent him over to be "broke in." That was five years ago, and Maggie had done many things for him since, but never in the bed. It just wouldn't be proper, considering how they felt about each other.

Dessa stepped quietly onto the balcony and peered down into the noisy room below. Before coming here, she never knew the difference between one saloon and another. But Rose had quickly set her straight.

Down at the Busted Mule a man could gamble and drink, but he came to the hurdy-gurdy house to dance with a pretty girl. Here he could still drink, in fact was encouraged to do so as well as buy his partner something. But he couldn't play a hand of poker. This was a dance hall, pure and simple. The cribs out back were something that Rose gilded over quickly. Dessa was pretty sure she knew what went on there, too, and the thought made her flush. At the same time, she wondered what it might be like to be with someone like Ben Poole. In one of the cribs. Without her clothes. Him naked, too.

She clapped a hand over her mouth. Of all things to think about. What had gotten into her, anyway?

Just as she leaned out over the balcony rail, Ben Poole, who had been ready to shove his way out of the batwing doors, turned to look upstairs and saw her there. He stopped cold right in the door and stared at her so long she wondered if something was wrong.

A whiskered man pushed his way past Ben, slapping up against him solidly. Ben stepped backward out of the way but didn't take his eyes off her. Then he smiled, tipped his hat, and moved through the doors and out into the darkening night.

Dessa pressed her lips together. Who did he think he was? She hadn't given him cause to acknowledge her in any way, that ignorant heathen. And him looking right up there at her, so everyone could see, and acting like they had a formal acquaintance. Rose might think highly of Ben Poole, but Dessa thought he was nothing but a no-account waster, a lazy frontier oaf. That story about him coming into town starving was sad, but it didn't change things. All a person had to do was pull himself up by his own bootstraps and work hard to be a success in this world. Hadn't her own daddy said so? And just because Ben Poole looked like one of those figures painted on the wall of a church didn't give him call to get familiar with her. Tip his hat at her so everyone in the place could see. She wasn't about to let her feminine emotions get the better of her where this man was concerned.

But he'd held her. Oh, how gently he'd held her, and she'd shed her tears on his flesh. That wasn't so easy to forget.

It was difficult getting through the night. Nightmares kept waking her just as she would drift off. More than once she fell, fell into the blankness of sleep and along would come the face of that horrible Coody; flames roared through her dreams, curling them at the edges, heating her so that she awoke drenched in perspiration, tears flowing. By morning she looked and felt utterly exhausted, and wondered how she would get through the funeral.

After a hurried wash in cold water from the pitcher beside her bed, Dessa dressed and slipped downstairs. Out in the street she found the town struggling awake. A few horsemen moved along, the shod hooves kicking up dust and echoing eerily in the quiet. The air was mountain clear and tinged with the sweetness of wildflowers. She breathed deeply and stared with awe at the high peaks cutting into the silver sky. Just to the right of one snowcapped tip, a star winked and went out. Tears lurking near the surface welled in her eyes, brought about not by grief but by a sight so achingly beautiful it transcended all earthly cares.

"Wonderful sight, isn't it?" a voice at her back said.

Startled, she turned to see Ben Poole lounging against the front of a building. "What are you doing here?"

"Same as you, I reckon. Claiming my piece of the walk, enjoying my piece of the heavens." He straightened and touched the brim of his hat but didn't remove it. "I trust you're doing fine, ma'am."

She swallowed hard. He made her feel twisted inside, like something wanted to happen but couldn't. She could only nod mutely, and he kept those bright blue eyes aimed right at her, one corner of his mouth turning up ever so slightly.

"Well, you take care of yourself, Miss Dessa Fallon," he said, and crossed the street, brushing so close to her she could smell leather and soap. Her heart pounded.

Mother once said you'd know. When you met the man you would love, you would know, and nothing would keep you from him. Nothing. But this couldn't be that knowing, could it? No, this was just grief and the feeling of loss, of desolation.

Yet, for some reason she wanted to run after him, pound at his back with her fists, and scream. Leave me be, she would shout. Don't do this to me, she would beg. But she didn't, because she knew that she really didn't want him to leave her alone, no matter what she might claim.

She would get through this day. She was strong and stubborn. Hadn't Mother always said so? Just like your father, she'd said.

"Oh, dear Lord, I hope so," Dessa murmured, then turned her back on the vanishing figure of Ben Poole and lifted her skirts to make her way to the dressmaker's, where a light glowed in the front window. Mrs. Fabrini, true to her word, was at work on final touches to the black dress. It fit perfectly.

When Dessa returned to the Golden Sun and stepped into her room carrying the brown paper parcel, she saw that steam rose from the half-filled bathtub. Bless dear Rose's heart. She knew just what Dessa needed. How would she ever repay the woman for all she had done for her? Somehow she would think of a way.

Bathed and dressed in Mrs. Fabrini's creation, she sat in front of the mirror struggling with her hair. It had suffered dreadfully from the experiences of the past few days. Normally she spent hours on her own ablutions, and shampooed and styled the long umber tresses frequently. Since her coming out last spring, she had taken to wearing her hair up in the fashion of a grown woman, not hanging loose and free like a child. But this morning she simply brushed the fly-away strands till they gleamed and put on the small black hat Mrs. Fabrini had taken upon herself to order from the milliner. With the filmy veil pulled down over her face, she felt sufficiently hidden from the curious stares that were sure to come her way.

After knocking softly, Rose entered the room. Dessa could see her in the mirror regarding her solemnly. Rose, too, wore black, and she was stunning. The blond hair and wide-brimmed lace hat set off her clear complexion and exquisite features. Dessa decided that no one could possibly tell by looking at her that Rose was the owner of a brothel.

"Walter is here to escort you, child," Rose said.

"Walter?"

"Sheriff Moohn. He insisted."

Dessa recalled the terse way in which the sheriff had informed her of her parents' death and wasn't sure she wanted to be on his arm during the funeral. She saw no way out of it, though, and so went with Rose downstairs. Their leather ankle-high shoes made dull echoes on the wooden floors still shiny and smelling of lye soap from their daily mopping.

Outside, a black carriage waited. Sheriff Moohn stood beside it, ready to help her into the seat. He climbed in and snapped the reins smartly onto the rump of a splendid black horse. A wagon waited on the street, two closed wooden coffins sitting side by side in the bed.

The sheriff and Dessa rode all the way to Boot Hill behind the wagon, not speaking. She didn't notice until they arrived that a great long procession followed them. Men, women, and children rode in wagons and carriages, others sat astride horses and a few mules, still others walked. It seemed to take forever for the crowd to make its somber way to the grave site on the slope of the hill.

Dessa had decided on holding the services out here in the open as the early sun splashed the valley with golden light. God's own cathedral, and it couldn't have been more beautiful. Reverend Blair, minister to the congregation of the raw-board church hastily finished for his arrival, had acquiesced to her wishes.

Moohn put his arm around Dessa's waist as the preacher began to speak, and she was suddenly very glad the gruff sheriff was there. Rose stepped in on the opposite side, and the two held her upright as well as together, for she feared she'd shatter in a hundred pieces.

Dessa stared at the coffins as long as she could, while the words of the preacher reached out to the crowd. Abruptly she felt as if someone were watching her, and raised her eyes. Through the riffling of the dark veil she saw, across the way near a grove of trees, a man moving into the open. A brief recognition caused her heart to flutter up into her throat. Something about his stance was oddly familiar. She squinted, trying to see his face, but he was too far away. He clutched a black hat in both hands in front of himself. A breeze tossed his thick crop of dark hair and the sun struck a startling white streak there.

For the slightest instant she thought the man was someone she knew, but that was ridiculous. It couldn't be. He reminded her of…She lost the thought, and lifted the veil to stare so hard at him that her vision blurred.

The stranger must have noticed, for he melted back into the shadows until she couldn't tell if he was even there. She shook away the uncomfortable feeling that she'd seen him somewhere before. Perhaps he would come to her after the services, when everyone would be expected to offer their condolences. She dragged her attention back to the preacher and, in the throes of her grief, forgot about the odd figure.

Moohn remained by her side as the entire procession of townspeople filed past. Each in turn clasped her hand briefly and murmured sympathies. At times Dessa thought her legs would just give way, that she wouldn't be able to stand there another minute. Then Rose would squeeze her hand reassuringly, and a new bit of strength would arise from down inside.

At last the end of the line drew near. And there, bringing up the rear, was Ben Poole. He had wet and combed his unruly long hair and was freshly shaved. He wore a cravat at the neck of his homespun shirt. The worn boots showed signs of having been polished at, even though the effort didn't seem to have done much good.

He looked down into her upturned face, his black-lashed blue eyes appearing to gaze right through the veil. Then he lifted her hand and kissed it gently. Before she could react in any way, he was gone. The feel of his hand holding hers, the warm spot where he had placed his lips, remained. She felt more comforted by his brief action than any words he could have spoken.

She asked to remain behind to be alone with her parents for a while, and Moohn and Rose Langue strolled discreetly a few paces away to stand beside the carriage and wait while she whispered her final good-byes.

Kneeling beside the caskets that would soon be lowered into the earth, Dessa thought of all her life spent with these two wonderful people. She refused to let her mind stray to what it would be like without them, but rather replayed over and over the happy times they'd had together. The years of laughter and tears, of joy and sorrow, of sharing and caring.

She could not mourn those, for they must sustain her for the rest of her life.

Dry-eyed she rose, patted her fingers gently on the rough pine boards, and, holding her head high, managed to walk without collapsing, back to where Moohn and Rose waited.

Five

After the funeral, Rose put Dessa to bed for the remainder of the day. The task proved easy. Dessa was totally exhausted by her ordeal and grief. Maggie peered in around noon carrying a tray, and found Dessa staring dry-eyed toward the draped windows.

"I brought you something to eat. Rose says I'm to stay and make absolutely sure you eat every bite."

Dessa rolled over on the silken sheet and faced her visitor. The petite woman had draped a gossamer satin robe over the scandalous red corset that pushed her small breasts up so they threatened to burst from the confines of the garment. Her tiny feet were bare, and the brunette tresses tousled, as if she hadn't brushed her hair yet. Surely Maggie had attended the funeral, but try as she might, Dessa couldn't recall a single face. No, that wasn't entirely true. She remembered Ben holding her hand up to his warm, velvety lips and gazing at her for a long moment, sadness darkening his intense blue eyes.

And the man in the woods with the streak in his hair. His image returned quite suddenly and vividly. Who was he and what did he want?

"Are you feeling okay? You've gone all white as a sheet," Maggie said, and placed the tray on the bedside table. Without waiting for a reply, she began to fluff pillows and stuff them behind Dessa. "Sit up. Eat. Or you'll face the wrath of Rose, and she's tough to cross."

Dessa did as she was told, smoothing the quilted comforter over her lap so Maggie could place the tray there. When Maggie lifted a towel off the food, a billow of aromatic steam fairly made Dessa's mouth water. She was surprised that she actually wanted to eat, and tackled the savory meat smothered in a thick brown sauce with chunks of potatoes and carrots. A hunk of bread lay on a separate plate. There was butter in a bowl, salt in its crystal cellar, and a fragrant cup of sweet tea. All were served on blue and white Bristow china.

Business must be good in bawdy houses.

Silently Maggie watched her devour the meal.

As Dessa swallowed the last bite, Maggie said, "There's apple pie, too, but I couldn't get it on the tray. It wouldn't do me to wait tables over at the Continental; I'd dump it all down someone's shirt front."

Dessa managed a weak smile at a vision of the red-corseted Maggie serving up meals at the chic eating establishment, her luscious breasts spilling out every time she bent to a table. The smile turned into a moan at the idea of eating anything else, even if it was her favorite dessert being offered.

"I couldn't eat another bite. I'm already stuffed. But apple pie? Maybe you could sneak me a piece for a snack tonight? That is, if I ever get over stuffing myself so. I can't think what got into me."

Maggie smiled with delight. "Plenty of good food, I'd say. I'll bring you a big slab of pie with a glass of milk later…uh, before we get too busy."

Spreading a hand over her bosom, Dessa tried not to think of what getting busy later that evening would mean to Maggie. Perhaps the girl only danced with those scruffy men who came into the Golden Sun, but somehow Dessa doubted it. In an effort to change the subject, she asked, "What was that wonderful stew?"

"Venison. It's the specialty of the house. Sometimes it's the only dish of the house." Maggie laughed at the look that crossed Dessa's face.

"Venison?"

"Deer, you know."

"Oh, dear, I think I do." Both giggled at her unintentional pun, before she continued. "I never thought I'd actually eat one of those lovely little creatures, though."

"Well, you didn't exactly eat the entire thing. Just a chunk or two." Maggie giggled again and took the tray, placing it back on the table. She plumped herself down on the edge of the bed, obviously eager to chat a while. "What do you eat? Back in Kansas City?"

"Beef. We eat a lot of beef and some pork. Goose and duck, pheasant sometimes. Chickens, too, and fish."

"Beef is a cow. What's the difference between that and deer?"

Dessa looked rueful. "Not as much as I thought."

Maggie chuckled, apparently quite enjoying their visit. "We eat fish here, too, when we can get one of the men to catch a mess. Tell me, what's it truly like back in the Americas?"

"Have you never been there?"

Maggie shook her head. "I barely remember. We came out with Brigham Young when I was little. I...I've been kicking around out here in the territories ever since."

"Well, I've lived all my life in Kansas City. The streets are lit with illuminating gas lamps. We can stroll in the park at night, down by the river. People drive around in marvelous carriages, landaus and runabouts and phaetons, some black with gold stripes. Very elegant and not at all like these chunky old wooden wagons out here. Last year Daddy had water piped into the house and installed a water closet. Not like here, where you either use the chamber pot or run out to the privy.

"We have servants who cook and clean and sew. Some of my friends have personal maids, but my daddy isn't quite that rich. He says we should take care of ourselves anyway, and now that I'm here, I see that he was right."

Dessa hadn't realized until she paused for breath that she spoke of that life, of her parents, as if she had only temporarily left it behind and could return whenever she wished. Harshly, hurtfully, she realized that she had not only lost her parents, she had lost that life. Perhaps not forever, for surely she could return home one day soon. But it would never be the same without them. She would have to carve out a new existence for herself. And everyone would expect her to marry right away. Oh, dear, what a terrible catastrophe.

Entranced, eyes shining with pleasure, Maggie encouraged her to continue her tale. "And what about dances? They have fancy balls, don't they?"

"Oh, yes, the ladies' gowns are beautiful, with yards and yards of tulle or taffeta. Some even wear the newest bustles and no crinolines. And the men dress in tight trousers, and shirts so white they dazzle the eye, and single-breasted waistcoats that plunge in the front. And the music is exquisite. The latest in polyphons with disk after disk of all the most popular songs.

"Just before I came out here to the frontier, we attended the summer cotillion at the Riverside Ball Room. I will never forget it—it was glorious. We danced the night away."

Maggie nodded. "And there must be plays. We have some plays here, too, at the opera house, and sometimes Rose takes one of us with her. Now that "he" isn't around anymore."

Though caught up in her own memories, Dessa couldn't

help but notice the accent Maggie put on that mysterious "he" in Rose's past. She had to admit to being somewhat curious about who the man Maggie spoke of could be and what had happened to him. The subject wasn't something she cared to discuss with Maggie, so she would remember to ask Rose when she knew her better.

A terrible clatter arose outside, bringing a halt to their chatter. Maggie jumped from the bed, drew back the heavy draperies, heaved open the window, and leaned out. The girl appeared to have no shame at all in exposing herself while half nude.

Her head still poked out the window, Maggie said to Dessa, "It's the posse, coming back empty-handed. I guess no one told you, they brought the bodies in yesterday. Held their funerals just after…well, uh…The men who were killed when the stage was robbed? Everyone is in a fair uproar. J.T. and Artie were both well liked. The vigilantes won't rest till they stretch the necks of those owlhoots, but sometimes I have my doubts about our good sheriff. He prefers checkers and Rose to carrying out the law."

Maggie turned from the window, hand over her mouth and eyes wide. "Oh, my goodness, I forgot. You saw them, didn't you? I mean, the men who did it. Rose said they dragged you off and would have done dreadful things to you and probably even killed you if you hadn't run off and found Ben."

"He's smitten with you, you know," Maggie finished with a giggle.

Dessa frowned. She was beginning to like Maggie despite her chosen occupation, but she didn't care to discuss Ben Poole with her or anyone else. Everyone in this place doted on him. She couldn't help wondering what they saw in him. She squeezed her eyes shut and felt again his strong but gentle arms enfolding her, his satin-smooth lips touching the back of her hand ever so tenderly

Angry at her own weakness, she mentally scolded herself. He was nothing but a useless and lazy frontiersman who would never amount to anything. One of those men who likes to play helpless so women will cater to him. Ben Poole was certainly not the kind of man a woman with her breeding should think twice about. And he never had anything worthwhile to say, if he chose to speak at all.

Maggie interrupted her ruminations. "Well, you could be nice to him. He really is a good person."

"I'm going down and find out what's going on. Rose says you're to stay in bed and get some rest, get your strength back. She'll be glad to see you ate your dinner."

Maggie grabbed up the tray and was gone before Dessa could say a word in her own defense about her feelings on the subject of Ben Poole.

Those feelings were reinforced later that afternoon when someone banged on the door a couple of times, then barged into her room. Half asleep, she lurched to a sitting position to see Ben Poole standing in the center of the room, big hands hanging loosely at his sides. His pants and shirt were powdered with dust and there was a sweaty ring around his golden hair where a hat had rested.

"Oh, I'm sorry, ma'am, I thought—"

"Get out!" she shouted, and tugged the covers up over the bodice of the gown she wore. Too skimpy, too lacy for her taste.

Ben backed up a step or two and grinned, looking like a kid caught at a pie set to cool on the window-sill. He hurriedly found his voice. "Seeing as how I'm here, I'll ask how you are before I go."

Enraged, she pointed past his shoulder. "Go, now! Get out of my room."

"By the sound of things, I guess you're better, or at least got your second wind. Glad to see your spirits haven't been dampened any."

Before Dessa could vent her rage at Ben's brash familiarity, Rose appeared in the open doorway behind him. "What in the thunder is all the shouting about? What are you doing to this girl, Ben?"

Turning to face Rose, Ben spread his palms and shrugged. "Not a thing, Rose. I just came in to—"

"He broke in on me while I was asleep, that's what. Scared me half to death. I'll thank him to leave my room this instant. He had no business—"

Ben smacked his chest with the flat of his hand, making a sudden hollow sound. "Tell me, don't tell her. I'm not deaf."

Dessa rose up onto her knees, forgetting to hold the covers over her bosom. "I did, and you just stood there like a—"

"Whoa, now. Both of you." Rose slipped past Ben, who looked as if he couldn't decide between getting an eyeful of Dessa in the thin gown or running for his life.

Rose solved the problem. "Stay right where you are, Ben. And you, child, will kindly not speak in that tone of voice. This is not your room; it belongs to me."

"But he—" Dessa sputtered, and realized that the silken gown was clinging to her nipples, which were rigid with the excitement of the moment. She scrabbled around to cover herself once again.

Ben managed to come to his own defense, but he couldn't tear his gaze from the flustered and angrily beautiful girl on the bed. "I thought Virgie was in this room, Rose. Tell her to stop yelling. I'm sorry I—"

"Both of you shut up, this instant. I never heard so much caterwauling in my life."

"He's looking for a fancy woman?" Dessa cried.

"Ben," Rose scolded.

"I didn't do anything."

"You came in my room without knocking, you...you lunkhead."

"I did not. I knocked. Hard. I did, Rose, I swear. You know I don't bust in on the girls."

"I'm not one of the girls," Dessa shouted.

"Hush, now, this instant, the both of you," Rose said, and shut the door on a crowd of curious onlookers gathered behind her.

As far as Dessa could see, the group was made up of half-clothed men and women. Instantly understanding what they were all doing just prior to her fracas with Ben, she wanted to crawl under something and hide.

Rose crossed both arms beneath her ample bosom. "Now settle down and we'll straighten this out." She indicated a straight-backed wooden chair. "Ben, sit. Dessa, behave yourself. You're acting like a spoiled child. I realize you've had a tough couple of days, but it's not Ben's fault. In fact, he's been more help than anyone, where you're concerned, and you need to recognize that."

"But I—"

Rose leveled a long finger at Dessa. "No! When I've finished."

Dessa clamped her lips shut. She only wanted to tell Rose that a decent woman did not have a man in her room while she was in bed, but obviously that didn't hold true in a brothel. She began to look around for an avenue of escape. It was entirely possible that Rose was setting her up for this clodhopper she was so fond of, and Dessa would have no part of it. Somehow she had to get out of here.

"Dessa, we offered you our hospitality, and we expect you to act like the lady you say you are. And Ben, you will apologize to Dessa for inadvertently barging into her room. She will be staying here for a few more days and I'd appreciate your remembering that and giving her the privacy she needs. Do you understand?"

Ben nodded, and then had the audacity to wink openly at Rose. The gesture infuriated Dessa. How dare the two of them talk around her as if she weren't there? They were the ones who didn't know how to behave properly.

"You go on to your fancy woman, sir," she said as sternly as her emotional state would allow. "And I will be out of this place just as soon as I can manage. I'm sorry if I have offended either of you with my manners." Her stern tone belied any penitence, but then to her horror she burst out crying and lost the advantage she imagined she had gained.

"Now look what you've done." Rose rushed to her side while chastising a befuddled Ben.

He gave them both a look that plainly said he would never understand women, and what's more, he wasn't sure he cared to, and then he slunk out of the room. The two of them had made him feel at fault for the entire episode, when all he'd wanted was for Virgie to give him a hot bath and rub his aching back with liniment.

Damn, that was the all-fired prettiest woman he'd ever seen, even when she'd slept and cried all day and didn't have any clothes on and her hair looked like a fly-away horse's mane. But he'd be blasted if he knew how to handle her. She had a mouth on her. That only made him admire her the more. There was no place in the territories for weakness. It was plain he was doomed to keep running into her in the most unexpected ways. And it was also plain that she'd as soon see him in hell as look at him.

Grumbling, Ben went in search of Virgie and his hot bath and massage, and maybe even something else, and to hell with them all.

Back in Dessa's room, Rose tried to comfort the crying girl. "It's all my fault, dear. Mine entirely. You've just been through so much and then I jump all over you some more. But please don't blame Ben."

Dessa dragged in a deep breath. Her eyes ached, her head pounded, and her throat felt raw. She had to stop this crying, and soon. And if people didn't quit defending Ben Poole to her, she was going to…well, she didn't know what she was going to do.

"He's like the old hound everybody in town feels sorry for and pets and feeds," she blurted to Rose. "And now he comes licking at my heels and I get in all kinds of trouble because I don't want to pet him, too."

Rose's mouth dropped open and she regarded Dessa for a moment before bursting out laughing. She whooped awhile, then slapped her thighs and whooped some more.

The hilarity, even though Dessa didn't think what she'd said was at all funny, proved catching, and after a while she laughed away her own tears.

When both women had calmed down, Rose gave her a big hug. "Now, you don't worry about how long you stay. Ben won't bust in here again, and neither will anyone else. When you feel ready, then you can decide what you want to do, but until then, you're welcome here. But honey, Ben is about as far from being an old hound as you'll ever find, and I think you'll learn that if you're around very long."

Dessa kept her silence, but she had no intention of getting any better acquainted with Ben, no matter how long she remained in Virginia City. The way he made her feel wasn't natural, and it frightened her. She'd been around men, been squired by the best, and had never experienced such a range of emotions as she did simply by being in the same room with him. It was terrifying. It must be that he awoke the animal in her. The one Mother always said was hidden in the best of females, the one that brought about feelings that must be held in check at all cost. Daddy had been a bit of a scalawag, had not always succeeded in taming his wilder side, but he was a man and that was to be expected. Women must control their baser desires, Mother would remind her often after she began to keep company with young men.

She had to be very careful indeed, for she might be just like her daddy, who on occasion had satisfied what she'd heard Mother refer to as his evil lust outside the marriage bed. A family secret mother shared with a few of her closest friends when she thought her daughter couldn't hear.

Dessa shuddered and snuggled deep under the luxurious covers. If she slept the rest of the day and night away, maybe things would look better come morning. Anyway, no one would think the worse of her for doing so after all she had been through.

Ben and Rose settled comfortably at a table where she could keep her eye on the entire dance floor so that no man might accidentally take advantage of one of her girls.

"Have any trouble on the trail today?" she asked over the foam-topped glass.

Ben glanced around, unable to keep his eyes from straying to the empty second-floor balcony and the closed door beyond. "Nope. Things have been pretty quiet since the killings. Must have scared them plumb to death. Walter have any idea who done it yet?"

"Hasn't said. Who do you reckon they were?"

Ben shrugged and downed half the glass of dark brew. "Yank's men, I'd say. But probably not the man himself. Being the kind of war hero some have made of him, I can't see him grabbing Dessa and trying to do her harm. The man may be wild as they come and willing to shoot a man who faces him off with a gun, but roughing up a woman? Not his style.

"In fact, I'd judge that he found out about those rascals' deed and did some punishing of his own. That may be the last we'll see of them around these parts."

Rose studied Ben intently. "You talk about him like you admire what he's doing."

"Nope. I just understand what the war did to men. No matter what side they were on."

"And you? What about you, Ben? What did the war do to you?"

He grinned in that lopsided way she so admired. "Hell, Rosie, you see me, what do you think?"

"I think men like Yank've got no excuse, not even the war, for robbing and killing, that's what I think. And you're proof of that."

His blue eyes clouded, flat as tarnished silver. "Since when am I so lily-white, Rose?"

"That wasn't your fault, Ben, and you dang well know it. When you gonna quit flailing yourself about it?"

Ben finished the beer and stood. "I quit doing that a long time ago, but I don't aim to forget my responsibilities, either."

Rose sighed and got rather stiffly to her feet. It had been a long day. 'You're a dear, sweet, stubborn boy, Ben Poole."

"And if I don't take myself off to bed, I'll be unemployed, too."

Ben reached the door and was putting his bedraggled hat on his head when a pale feminine face appeared in the darkness peering over the batwing doors. It so startled him that he jerked backward a few paces.

"Is Miss Rose there?" the woman asked in a wobbly voice.

Dumbstruck, Ben nodded. He recognized her, and wondered what the wife of Preacher Blair was doing out on the street this late at night. More important, what was she doing coming around the Golden Sun Saloon and requesting a meeting with its proprietor? Ben wasn't sure he wanted to stick around to find out, but his curiosity was such that he could no more leave than walk naked down the street at high noon.

"Please fetch her for me," Molly Blair ordered, her words crisper now as she gained courage.

"Yes, ma'am," Ben murmured, and backed up a few paces, bumping against a table. He righted a teetering chair and looked around for Rose. Seeing her behind the bar, he motioned.

Rose pointed at her own midsection and gave him one of those Who, me? looks. Ben nodded, darted a glance back toward the batwings to make sure he hadn't been seeing a mirage, then beckoned impatiently. The pale, moon-shaped face was still there, looking strangely as if it hung suspended all on its own.

Rose finally strolled over. She gave Ben a second look that told him she thought he had taken leave of all his good sense.

"Mrs. Blair is out yonder. Wants to talk to you."

"Who?"

"Mrs. Blair, Preacher Blair's wife. You know,, Rose. The Virginia City Congregational Church."

Rose self-consciously touched her hair and straightened her low-cut dress. "What do you suppose she wants?"

"I don't know, but if you don't go see, I'm just going to go right up to her and plain ask. One thing's for sure. She don't want to dance."

Ben followed on Rose's heels as she made her way toward the waiting woman. He overheard almost all of Mrs. Blair's curt request.

"...outside here a moment, I would like a word with you."

"Well," Rose said quite loudly, and pushed open one of the double doors, "Why don't you come right on in and join me in a drink?"

Ben flinched. That wasn't what Rose should have said.

Molly Blair drew herself up stiffly. "I should say not."

She was a plain little thing, as one expected a preacher's wife to be; her sandy hair was pulled so tightly into a bun toward the top of her head that the corners of her small eyes slanted upward. Nothing about her, thought Ben, was remarkable except perhaps the primness of her lips and a flaring of her rather wide nostrils. Even if it were allowed, she wouldn't have been pretty.

"Well, then, Mrs. Blair," Rose boomed, "I'd say that if you refuse to come into my place of business, then we haven't anything to say to each other."

The nostrils made ready to spout flames. "Then I'll say my piece from this very spot, madam. I...we ladies of the church intend to see that Virginia City is cleared of establishments like yours and the riffraff it attracts. We want to make this town a safe place for decent folk to live in. A place where we don't have to cover our children's eyes and ears when we walk with them down the street. It's time you and your fancy women were run out."

Molly Blair delivered the entire speech looking past Rose's shoulder, her hazel eyes hard with disgust. Ben felt like dodging the glare, standing as he was a little to the right of her aim and at Rose's back.

When the altercation had started, everyone in the hurdy-gurdy house stopped what they were doing. Even the tinkle of music from the Cremona had faltered and died. No one appeared willing to wind it back up. Dancers gathered in a scraggly line at the edge of the sawdusted floor, their partners gaping openly at the unusual conflict. A showdown between Rose and Preacher Blair's mousy wife might get more interesting than shuffling around in circles hoping for a fleeting touch of feminine flesh.

Even the Golden Sun's unflappable bartender, Grisham, was stricken dumb at the site of Miss Rose standing still for a tongue-lashing from Molly Blair.

zzThe piano was rewound, the bartender went back to drawing beer from the wooden kegs under the bar, and Rose planted her hands on her hips and whirled on Ben, her cheeks flushed redder than the paint on them.

"What in the thunder was that all about?"

He fiddled with his hat a moment, then finally screwed it back on his head. "I'd say you got yourself a battle to fight. But I wouldn't worry too much about it. She's pretty frail. Up beside you, she won't stand a chance."

"Get out of here, Ben Poole. Go crawl underneath your wagon and tuck that smart-aleck face down under the covers before I yank one of your ears off. Go on, git!"

Ben laughed heartily as he crossed the street and headed for the freight yard and his bed. He predicted that Rose would make short shrift of Molly Blair and her bunch of do-gooders. It might be a battle worth watching.

Six

The steady chime of a church bell awoke Dessa the next morning. She'd forgotten what day it was, perhaps even where she was, until that very moment when she lifted her head and gazed out the window toward the distant mountain peaks. No one had closed the drapes the night before and she was glad, for the blue sky and clean bright sunshine began her day quite nicely.

She was filled with a vague sense of relief that the funeral was over and done with. Maybe that was the reason society insisted on such an arduous death ceremony. It cleansed the heart and soul, finalized the most senseless loss in a civilized way. She wanted suddenly to attend church and complete the ritual circle.

After a quick wash, she fingered the black funeral dress hanging over the back of the chaise. It would do. But the underthings were another matter. After due consideration, she managed to don the shameful silken underwear, but absolutely couldn't bring herself to consider the black, lacy, totally disreputable corset. Not in church. Not even if no one could see it.

She dangled it in one hand and remembered how she'd looked yesterday when Rose bound her up in the thing. Why, it had shoved her breasts almost up under her chin. There'd been no strength to object when she was being dressed for the funeral, and certainly not to that bull-headed Rose. But Rose wasn't here today.

Dessa shook her head and made up her mind. She simply couldn't make herself put the skimpy thing on. She dropped it on the bed and wondered fleetingly if the wicked garment might belong to Virgie, the girl Ben Poole was looking for when he had burst into her room. Did he like his women to wear things like that?

"Oh, pooh." She slipped the dress down over her head and buttoned the bodice.

Settled in front of the mirror, she brushed at the long curly tangles of hair and thought how wickedly good it felt not to have the bindings of a corset inhibiting her every movement and breath. She hadn't imagined the freedom of such a thing until she actually tried it. And even better, no crinolines to make her dress stand out all around like an enormous balloon. It seemed not to be the style out here in the territories, where practicality had to come first. Nor had she seen even one of the newfangled bustles that were all the rage in Kansas City. Secretly she thought the bustle a sensible replacement for the ungainly crinoline with its laced ribs.

Perhaps on the frontier women weren't so starchy about what they wore. She must ask. The thought made her blush, however, since the only women she knew worked at the Golden Sun. Perhaps their opinion wouldn't be the best to judge by.

Leaving her dark, fly-away tresses hanging loose, she found the slippers she'd borrowed and the black hat she'd worn the day before, and rushed from the room. If she didn't hurry, she'd miss the services.

What a rowdy and improper girl Mother and Father would think her, running off late for church without even a pin in her hair and improperly attired. Thinking of her parents threatened to bring tears, but she batted her eyelids and swallowed down the thick burning sensation. Not today. Today would begin the life she must salvage, and it absolutely could not start with crying.

At the top of the staircase, intent on keeping the hat on her head and hitching up the long dress, she took a step down and bumped right into Ben Poole.

He grasped her arms to steady her. "Oops, I beg your pardon, ma'am."

She impaled him with an icy gaze. "Can't wait to get to your fancy woman, Mr. Poole?" Immediately, she wished she could take back the words. The very idea. Letting him see that she even cared what he was up to.

He swept his hat off and bowed from the waist. "You are about the fanciest woman I know." Then he tripped on up the stairs, chuckling maddeningly.

She vowed she wouldn't look, but she did. Stopped right there, squeezing the banister until her knuckles were white, and turned to watch him stride the length of the balcony. Muscles rippled, tightening the threadbare shirt across his back. She wanted to reach out to him, but didn't.

Ben had a hard time walking away from her and that's why he almost ran. What had come over him anyway? Touching her like that, tipping his hat and actually exchanging such flippant words. They had just spilled from his mouth like he had no control at all over himself.

Tapping at the door of Rose's room, he balanced on the balls of his feet as if readying for a race. The girl made him jumpy as hell. Made him feel like he was filled up with something hot and fuzzy that needed to escape and the only way it could was for him to leap and shout and roll about.

Rose called for him to enter and he slipped inside, still thinking about Dessa and how lovely she looked with her hair hanging down around her shoulders, a dark frame for her delicate features. And that one hand up trying to hold her hat on so that her breasts poked at the black fabric of her dress.

"Where's she going so early?" he asked.

"Well, good morning to you, too, Ben." Rose smiled sweetly.

"Oh, sorry. Good morning."

Rose nodded and motioned him to the small table in front of a sunlit window. "Join me for breakfast?"

Ben eyed the plate of thin pastries and the china teapot painted with pink roses. "You call this breakfast? She going to church, you reckon?" He slipped into the dainty chair and ate three of the little pastries in one big bite.

"Of all the things I've tried to teach you, instilling some manners would seem to be my biggest failure."

'These are pretty good, but there's not enough here for both of us. I'd better git on over to the Continental and order me up some hash browns and eggs and biscuits and ham and—"

"The day you eat at the Continental will be the day pigs fly, and that'll be quite enough of your foolishness, Ben."

He grinned lopsidedly. "Yes, ma'am." He sucked at a tooth. "She okay today?"

Rose laughed. "Why, Ben. If I didn't know better, I'd think you were smitten. I thought you wanted absolutely nothing to do with Dessa Fallon, and here you are. Can't even stay off the subject for one full minute, not even to talk about food. Just what's going on?"

"Aw, hell, Rosie, I don't know. What is going on? My best intentions are to cross the street when I see her coming, yet I bull right up in her face every chance I get. That's the all-fired prettiest woman I've ever seen."

"You've seen plenty of pretty women around here. There's more to it than that, and don't think I don't know it."

"Well, there may be, but I don't know what it is, I swear I don't. She isn't going to give me the time of day, and why should she? Look at me, Rosie. And look at her. Even with not a stitch to call her own, all red-eyed and swole up from grieving her parents, she's pretty as a field of daisies nodding their shiny white heads in the sunlight. That girl's had a hold on me since I carried her in out of the dark of night all bruised and battered."

"I wish you'd tell me how to get out of this. I've thought of just riding off and not coming back, but there's ties here I can't break and I just won't do that. I keep hoping she'll up and leave, and things will get back to normal, but she's not showing any signs of that."

"What do you think, Rosie, what do you think?"

"I think you're smitten, just like I've already said. And the best cure for that is to just walk right up to the girl and tell her so."

Ben's eyes bugged. "Aw, no. I couldn't. She'd probably knock me a windin'."

Rose chuckled. "Well, of course not in so many words. Make your move, see where you stand. If she keeps pushing you away, then you'll just have to get over her. But you know something, I'm not so sure she will.

"She's a spoiled little thing and a lot younger than her age. That's from being overly protected and pampered by her rich folks. She can overcome that, given the right inspiration."

"Well, hell, Rose, I've never been anybody's inspiration, now, have I?"

Rose sobered and gazed at Ben, remembering the first time she'd seen him, standing at her door, hat in hand, the package in his fist that Ramey had sent over from the Busted Mule.

She shook her head, steered her thoughts back to Ben. He'd grown a lot since that day five years ago, put on weight from the good food, and lost his haggard appearance. The haunted eyes that had seen so much death at such an early age had cleared since he'd come to Virginia City, his own death nipping at his heels. And she'd grown to love him like a son. But she did wish she could teach him not to take life so seriously, not to take himself so seriously. That episode with Sarah's husband had been tragic, and no way out of it. But he did so need to get past it. Until he did, she feared he'd have no life to call his own. This unexpected interest in Dessa Fallon might just turn the trick.

Things came, they went. You had to reach out and grab a taste, lest you missed everything life had to offer. And so what if that taste was all you got? Something else would come along.

"Ben, you just don't know what inspiration you've been to this old lady."

Ben leaped from the chair, unable to sit still another minute. "You, an old lady? Why, shame on you, Rosie." He leaned down and kissed her powdery dry cheek. "Love you, old lady," he whispered, and bounded from the room, slamming the door so that it made Rose's eyes blink and release the tears standing there.

Dessa walked backward after she got downstairs, wondering what Ben was doing up there and who he was doing it with. Virgie, she supposed. The idea made her cringe. And why on earth did she care anyway? He was an uneducated man with no promise of a future. He'd probably get killed some dark night out in the mountains riding on top of that freight wagon, and no one would even know it for days. How awful, how absolutely awful to have no family. If she didn't watch out, she'd get to feeling sorry for him, and then where would she be? It occurred to her, as if she'd been hit broadside, that she was now in the same position as Ben Poole. Neither had kith or kin.

Oh, Dessa, get yourself on to church before you miss everything but the closing hymn. And stop thinking of that unschooled heathen who wears his hat in the house and probably burps at the table.

She imagined the domestic scene of she and Ben sharing a meal. He would lean back so his britches stretched tightly across his stomach and burp softly behind one of those big capable hands, and look across at her with vivid blue eyes outlined in black lashes.

Stop that, Dessa, right this instant!

She bounded through the door. Out on the boardwalk, she glanced up and down the street. The church was back up the way Ben and Wiley had brought her into town, and she headed in that direction. Only a few people were on the street. She passed an alley in which there sprawled an old, white-whiskered man. Sleeping off a drunk, she supposed. She met a bearded, rotund gentleman who tipped his hat and walked on.

Lifting her skirts, she descended a few steps off the walk into the street and cut across toward the rather innocuous wooden building with its small bell tower. The double doors were open, and from inside came the sounds of the congregation singing mightily. Obviously folks around here made up for their plain appearance by being robust in their worship. She slipped inside and into a back pew just as they finished singing the opening hymn and rustled and clattered into their seats.

She settled in and gazed at her surroundings. A wide plank floor, so new it smelled of freshly cut wood, hanging kerosene lamps, rugs leading to the altar. The wooden pews were plain and handcrafted. There was an organ up front and on the wall above the altar was written, "Glory to God in the highest and on earth peace."

Peace. How wonderful.

She took a deep breath and felt a certain peace, sitting there waiting for the preacher to begin.

He approached the lectern and she leaned forward in anticipation.

At that moment someone whispered in her ear, "Excuse me. Is this seat taken?" The speaker's breath feathered warmly over her cheek, and she turned to look right into the earnest face of Ben Poole. Their noses almost brushed. For a split second neither moved or blinked. Then she caught her lower lip in her teeth and leaned backward to escape the warmth exuding from his shiny, scrubbed countenance. Idly she wondered why he wore no facial hair, as was the style of most men. At first she had thought him perhaps no older than her, but now she could see tiny wrinkles at the corners of his eyes and minute tracks from the finely sculpted nostrils down to the corners of his generous lips. Noticing her attention, he lifted those lips into a tentative smile.

"Well?" he asked.

The woman seated in front of Dessa tossed a quick, obviously irritated glance over her shoulder.

"Sit and be still," Dessa said, and bundled the black skirt up against one hip.

He slid in beside her, crossed one leg over the other, and placed his hat on his knee. The next thing she knew, he had leaned his lips up right against her ear and said, "Yes, ma'am, I'll do that. And I thank you for reminding me of my manners."

She suppressed a smile.

Ben wondered what in the world he was thinking of. All along he had been sure that the best thing for him to do was to stay far away from Dessa Fallon, and here he was just plain daring her to be nice to him. Begging her to pay attention, when he knew what he should do was run the other direction as if his tail were on fire and her with more matches.

Still, maybe it wouldn't hurt to try out Rose's suggestions. She was right some of the time, especially when it had to do with men and women.

All he knew for sure was that ever since he'd barged into Dessa's room at the Golden Sun and got an eyeful of her in her nightgown in bed, he'd been acting crazy, at least in his head. And now here he was picking at her like they were in the first stages of courting. Him who had never courted a woman, least of all an upstanding one like her. Well, he wouldn't let it get too serious, that was all. He'd just have a little fun, then back off before she could smack him one across the head. He enjoyed the way her eyes sparked fire from their green depths when he annoyed her. Like coals burned down there. She was the first female he'd ever enjoyed actually being around in a man/woman kind of way. It felt good, and definitely not the same as being with Rose or Maggie. He decided to take advantage of it, short run that it might prove to be. Dessa would never let it go on very long anyway, and why should she?

She had never been as conscious of the presence of anyone as she was of Ben sitting so close to her. He smelled of shaving soap and saddle leather, all mixed up with an earthy aroma she couldn't quite identify. His large frame seemed to fill in all the spaces around her, and he emanated a sensual heat that was very pleasant and disconcerting.

She didn't hear a word of the sermon, and after the closing hymn was sung, Ben stepped past her into the aisle and let her move out in front of him. He then cupped her elbow with one hand just as if they were a couple and walked her outside, where they stood in the brilliant late morning sunlight studying each other intently. The spell was finally broken when a few of the young married women dragged their husbands over to introduce themselves to Dessa and again voice their condolences over the death of her parents. They were all very friendly with Ben, and he with them. It was easy to see that everyone liked him.

The glorious day, kissed by a cooling breeze off the distant mountains, overpowered any inclination Dessa might have had to become depressed. It was much too lovely a day.

And as if reading her mind, Ben, who stood quietly at her side, leaned down and said softly, "It's a beautiful day. Do you ride?"

"Yes, of course, but I—"

"Rose has a pair of blacks that need exercise. I usually take them out on Sundays and give them a good run. Come with me."

She gazed at a glint of sunlight off a distant snowcapped peak that jutted into the crystal-blue sky. Imagined riding beside him across a meadow, wind blowing through her hair. Blowing through his.

"I don't have a riding dress."

"If you did, would you go?"

She looked up into his blue eyes, as brilliant as the sky, and nodded. Yes, she would. And probably rue the day, but yes, she would, and she told him so.

Less than an hour later they rode out of town up the rise toward Boot Hill, Dessa clothed in a borrowed riding outfit and sitting in Rose's gleaming leather sidesaddle. She glanced quickly toward the raw mounds of earth where her parents had been buried the day before, then looked away.

Ben didn't say anything until they turned their mounts and headed into the glorious afternoon. 'You'll miss them, but they loved you."

She glanced quickly at him, saw that indeed the wind was tousling his shaggy hair, just as she'd imagined, blowing it back from the sun-bronzed forehead and jaw line to reveal well-formed ears with large lobes. A fine sheen of sweat glistened on the chiseled features.

Abruptly he returned her look and she turned away, embarrassed to have been caught studying him so closely. There were things about him that surprised her, and she wanted to figure them out. But doing so might lead to something she was afraid she couldn't handle. Like a physical attraction. At eighteen, she had just begun to taste of the sexual play between men and women. She knew flirting, enjoyed casual touching like lips brushing the back of a hand, a joining of palm to waist during a dance. No man had ever gone any further than a casual goodnight kiss, and that was only from Andrew. She could see that Ben might do more, and she might let him. But she had no notion why.

The black that Dessa rode—Baron was his name—was a spirited gelding with an arched neck and delicate legs and feet, not much like the sturdier mounts most horsemen preferred for the mountains. Ben rode its perfect match, a feisty mare called Beauty. She didn't seem to know her companion had been gelded and tossed her head to show off for him, prancing sideways and occasionally rubbing shoulders in a coquettish way. It embarrassed Dessa, but only because of where the flirtatious actions sent her own imagination. Ben Poole was paying court to her, whether he knew it or not.

"Here, you silly female," Ben scolded once when the mare actually moved so close that he and Dessa rubbed legs. "She thinks she can tempt him even though he—" Ben broke off, realizing that he shouldn't refer to animal sexuality in front of this girl. He saw why Rose despaired of ever teaching him good manners.

Dessa laughed. "She's just doing a little harmless flirting. He doesn't have to be equipped to enjoy that, surely."

"You are a bold little thing, aren't you?" Ben asked.

"Bold? Oh, you mean about the gelding. We had a lot of animals when I was growing up. Their behavior is a fact of nature, and nothing to be embarrassed about. Ben Poole, I do believe you're blushing."

He took off his hat and rubbed an arm across his forehead. "It's just the heat. I thought you were a city girl, brought up in Kansas City, you said."

"Well, in a way. Daddy built us a large house when he began to make money with the business, but it was out in the country. Later we had a place in town, too, where we'd live in the winter. I liked the farm, but Mother preferred living in the city. We had a little of both."

He nodded, reined the mare up. "Yonder, down through the trees, is a creek and some shade. Let's ride down and get a drink. It's getting mighty hot in this sun."

Dessa admitted to that, but questioned how wise it might be to ride off the main trail. "I thought you were supposed to exercise the horses."

Ben studied her tilted head a moment, then kicked at Beauty's ribs. "Across the meadow and back again. Come on, let's go." His shout vibrated through the hot afternoon, and Dessa kicked Baron into motion, maneuvering in the tricky sidesaddle when the gelding took off.

By the time they reached the edge of the meadow, they were neck-and-neck. Ben turned the surefooted mare, clods flew from under her hooves, and Dessa leaned into the turn and followed.

Wind dried the perspiration trickling from under her heavy hair; the gelding's shoulder and neck muscles gleamed. She smelled the animal's sweat and the freshly churned grasses and soil, and then the sweet, damp odor of water as they neared the end of their race, back where they'd started. Beauty won by half a head.

Laughing, Ben leaped from the horse before she came to a complete standstill, captured Baron's bridle, and let Dessa dismount on her own. She did so with agility.

"Not by much, you didn't win," she said, looking up into his openly joyful face. He almost became someone else when he loosened up and laughed. Another person, the one she'd only sensed earlier, came out from behind the frosty blue eyes.

"No, not by much. But a win is a win."

"And me on a sidesaddle, too. Too bad you didn't bet anything."

"Like what?" he asked, and began walking through the trees toward the sound of flowing water.

Dessa slipped off the pair of buttery riding gloves Rose had insisted she use to protect her hands, and walked along beside Ben, taking two steps to his one. They entered a shady glen and the temperature dropped a few degrees. She smelled mosses and wet earth and last year's leaf fall.

A gentle breeze tickled the thick foliage.

She lifted her hair off her neck. "Ah, that feels good."

He eyed the perky rise of her breasts and quickly looked away. It might have been a very bad idea, coming to this remote spot with a woman he felt so drawn to.

He cleared his throat and strolled on, keeping his eyes off his companion. At the edge of the creek he dropped the reins of both horses. Together the blacks stepped delicately into the water and began to drink. She watched them for a few moments. They were absolutely beautiful, long of leg, shanks rippling with muscle, taut bellies, and flowing manes and tails. There in the hidden glen surrounded by enormous trees and trailing brush and the splatter of sunlight, the perfectly matched pair made quite a picture indeed. How cruel the male couldn't fulfill his nature.

Ben watched Dessa. While he was conscious of the backdrop that she so much admired, what he looked at was her. The gold riding outfit that Rose had lent her accented her dark hair and pale skin. She looked much like a hothouse flower unexpectedly blooming in an untamed wilderness.

Then she turned and met his gaze. A patch of sunlight flickered in his hair. She licked her lips and took a step toward him, fascinated by the glowing halo around his head. Her heart kicked at her ribs when he moved toward her. In a moment, in just one more moment, they would touch. And she wanted that, reached out for it tentatively.

He took her fingers in his, leaned forward, and kissed the tip of each one. His lips were warm and moist, sending tingles all the way up her arm and straight to the sensitive tips of her breasts. She took a very deep breath, and instead of pulling away, moved a little closer.

He slanted a glance up through his astounding dark lashes, then lifted his head even with hers. She leaned forward ever so slightly and their mouths brushed as fleetingly as feathers in a breeze.

She batted her eyes and sucked in a lungful of air, and he turned loose of her fingers and put a little more space between them. She touched her own lips, still watching him but seeing that he stared at the ground somewhere between them.

"Ben?"

He began to shake his head vigorously back and forth, but he didn't say anything.

Her breasts pressed rigidly against the silken underwear that belonged, she thought, to Virgie, and between her legs a pulsating warmth grew. It felt so wonderful and so naughty she could hardly stand still.

He put the back of his hand against his mouth, then held it out to study the skin as if he could see remnants of the gentle kiss outlined there.

"Oh, Ben," she breathed.

"No," he said sharply. "I'm sorry. It's my fault. I didn't mean to do that. Rose always says I don't have any manners, and that's all that was. A lack of manners.

He felt ashamed of his pulsating desire, even more ashamed that he had let it show. She was young and innocent, probably not experienced at all in things like this. Now he had her all wide-eyed and confused, and he would have to hurt her to put a stop to it. Or maybe, like he'd thought before, she was only toying with him.

He turned his back on her, fetched the horses with a kissing sound. Looking back at the expression on her face, he saw that he already had hurt her with the explanation, the denial of his need.

Well, that was best.

He reclaimed the hanging reins. "Come on, you lunkheads, you'll bloat." His voice sounded angry, and he could see that hurt her more, but he couldn't help it.

"Want a drink before we go?" he asked, holding the gelding's reins out to her.

"Yes," she stammered, and fell down on her knees at the water's edge. She splashed the icy snowmelt up over her face and neck, gasping. After drinking from cupped hands, she arose and took the leather reins without looking at him.

They walked back to the trail single file, not talking at all. He went first, so that she had to stare at the haunches and swishing tail of his mare all the way out.

Seven

Rose had problems of her own the afternoon Ben and Dessa went riding, for Molly Blair accosted her right out on the boardwalk as she took her afternoon stroll. Still dressed in her Sunday best, Mrs. Blair epitomized a preacher's wife. She wore a plain brown frock, obviously inexpensive, with a matching bonnet properly tilted to shadow her face. The toes of her polished black shoes barely peeked from beneath the hem of her skirt. Her long, rather bony face wore an expression that warned she was armed for battle. So did the parasol she shook in the direction of Rose's midsection.

Rose's inclination was to yank the sunshine-yellow parasol from her own shoulder and use it as a defensive weapon. A picture of two women dueling with parasols on the streets of Virginia City on a sleepy Sunday afternoon tickled her fancy, and she couldn't help grinning.

Molly Blair was having none of it. Splotches reddened her angry features. "One of your girls was in our church this morning. Sitting right there in the front pew as bold as brass."

"I should think you would be pleased," Rose offered, not knowing what else to say. She couldn't think who the woman was talking about. Probably Maggie. Occasionally she had an attack of religion. But to sit in the front pew? She'd best talk to her about it.

"Pleased? Pleased?" Molly Blair bawled.

Spittle sprayed Rose, but she held her ground. "Please control yourself."

"It isn't I who can't control myself. Do you think we want those dirty, filthy fancy women darkening the door of our...of our Lord's church?"

Rose didn't miss a beat. "I believe He welcomed them, didn't He?"

Molly Blair narrowed her eyes and took a deep breath. Rose thought for a moment she would swing the parasol at her, club her over the head for daring to know the Good Book. Instead the woman shuddered in a most unattractive way and continued in a soft hiss.

"You keep your mouth off our Lord. I warned you that this town has to be rid of such as you and your kind. I'll not give you another warning. We will see Virginia City a fit place to raise children."

Rose wondered who we was, since no one seemed to be accompanying the woman, but she didn't ask. What a pity such a young woman found it necessary to make life so terrible for herself and those around her. Seeing her this way, Rose understood why Preacher Blair always looked so dour, like he'd had his nose down in the vinegar jar.

Rose decided against battle, and said sweetly, "It's been so nice talking to you, Mrs. Blair. I hope we meet again. Perhaps you'd care to come to my place for a cup of tea. Do bring the reverend with you. I have some marvelous biscuits from London that I'm sure you and your husband would enjoy."

Rose twirled her frilled yellow parasol, angled it over one shoulder, and strode off, bidding the woman good day in a bright, controlled voice. An explosion was about to occur and she wanted to be out of range.

Ben and Dessa rode past Rose a few seconds later, he and

Beauty several paces in front of Dessa and Baron, and both riders staring forward as if alone.

Rose watched the couple dismount at the livery and turn the horses over to the stable boy. She wondered what in the world was wrong with those two. They walked stiffly away from each other as if they might catch some dread disease if they lingered. She supposed Ben had gone and put his foot in his mouth again. She'd have a talk with him. On the other hand, maybe it was Dessa who needed the talking to. The poor child hadn't much of a good-sense upbringing, thinking that everything happened either to cause her pleasure or pain. In that respect she was more like a child of ten or twelve than a grown woman.

Rose hurried to catch up with Dessa, but the girl was stomping along at such a frenetic pace she was inside the Golden Sun and halfway up the staircase before Rose could catch her.

"Dear child, where are you going in such a rush? What happened?"

Dessa just kept moving, stumbling on the top step and fairly running into the room Rose had so generously let her use. The door slammed in Rose's face, and she twisted the knob angrily, throwing it back open.

"The very idea, Dessa Fallon. Where are your manners?"

Dessa whirled, features furrowed and stern. "Don't you start telling me what a fine man Ben Poole is or I swear I'll be sick!"

"Here, now, calm yourself down. No matter what has happened, you've no call to be so inconsiderate. Now sit down and tell me what Ben has done this time."

Dessa glared at Rose for a moment. Done? Done? What had he done? Nothing, and that was the problem. He'd brushed her off, just as smoothly as you please. But how could she tell Rose that?

"Well," Rose said, tugging off her yellow gloves and depositing them along with the parasol on the bed, "don't tell me he took advantage of you."

Dessa laughed harshly. "Not hardly. No, he didn't take advantage of me. Quite the opposite."

Rose stared at her a moment. Then the light dawned. "The opposite? You threw yourself at young Ben and he didn't want to play? Oh, child, how perfectly awful for you. And so now you're very angry and think you've been right all along about his unsuitability for such as you?"

Dessa threw herself down on the bed. "No…yes…I don't know. Oh, Rose, I'm not sure what's going on. I feel very strange when I'm around Ben. I know that he and I are worlds apart. We don't think alike, we don't want the same things, and we certainly have nothing in common. But he is so…so…oh, I don't know."

Rose sat beside the distraught girl and put an arm around her rigid shoulders. "Yes, indeed, Ben is so…and there's no word for it, is there? Well, there is a word for the way you're feeling, and you might just stop fighting it and let things happen naturally."

Dessa sighed. "Oh, yes, there is a word. It's whispered in drawing rooms when men think women aren't listening. It's lewd and disgusting, and I know I should be ashamed of myself for feeling this way."

"Men. I've been around a lot of men this summer, and none of them…I mean, my crowd, we would have a little fun, laugh and tease and run away and run back. And it was all so innocent. Then I come out here to this wilderness and the first thing that happens is I get caught up in the arms of that silent blond giant and I go all soft and gooey inside and I can't think straight and everything comes apart. And all he does is look at me with those big blue eyes. So serious but so distant, like he's not even seeing me." She put her hands over her face and dissolved in tears."

Rose pulled her close and smoothed strands of damp hair from the girl's face. "Lewd and disgusting indeed. Oh, sweet dear one, it's not so tragic to fall in love, it really isn't. Oh, sometimes it'll hurt like the very devil, but other times will make up for that, believe me. You'll know rapture such as you can't imagine."

"I'm…not…in…love," Dessa sobbed.

"Oh, that's what you think," Rose murmured. Then she added decisively, "Now stop this nonsense, wash your face and comb your hair, and let's go to supper. You'll feel better."

With the sweet-scented cloth from the washstand, Dessa scrubbed at her skin and dragged in a ragged breath. Suppose Rose was right. What would she do then? She really hadn't even decided what she would do about Andrew, the business, or returning to Kansas City, now she had to consider what she would do if she were falling in love with Ben Poole. Oh, what a mess. One thing piled right upon another, without a chance to take a breath. If this was what it was like to be an adult, then she wanted no part of it.

She had been so excited at her coming-out ball only last April. Prepared to take on the duties of a full-grown woman. To consider beaus and pick the one most suited to her family's lifestyle. Get engaged, marry, have children, run a household. Now look at her. Perhaps she should return to Kansas City and tell Andrew she would marry him. What other choices were there for a young woman without a family? If only Mitchell were alive. He always knew what was best for her.

An unbidden image caught her totally by surprise. A memory of the man who had lurked in the edge of the woods during her parents' funeral.

Thinking of him, she held the cloth over her face for another minute. Why did she feel so odd, as if something were about to happen that she'd been expecting all along? She shook her head and folded the cloth across the rim of the china bowl.

Turning to Rose, she asked, "Do you suppose there would be a home here I could rent for a while? I mean, if I decided to remain in Virginia City?"

Rose smiled with satisfaction. "I wouldn't be a bit surprised. Just what do you have in mind? Perhaps we could talk about it over our meal. I don't know about you, but riding out with a man always left me famished."

She cast a sly look toward Dessa and almost burst into laughter at the flush that spread over the younger woman's throat and face.

"We didn't...I wouldn't—"

"Well, of course not, child. Isn't that what you said? Well, maybe not quite. You said he wouldn't, but then it's almost the same thing, isn't it?" Rose might have treated the matter lightly, but she was quite concerned about this young woman, who, she would bet her bottom dollar, had never been with a man. She vowed to speak with Ben very soon.

Dessa trailed along behind Rose across the balcony and down the stairs and out the swinging doors. The beautiful dance hall owner was more outspoken than anyone Dessa knew. Nothing seemed to faze her in the least, and she would joke about anything she pleased. It was taking some getting used to, but it must be the way of people in the territories.

Daddy had said that only the very roughest and strongest made their way out here. Of course, he was speaking of businesspeople, but it must hold with everyone. Men and women alike. Dessa would like to think she was strong and tough enough to forge a life in this untamed place. Or was she only being romantic? Getting along on her own would be hard anywhere, but more so here. Women just naturally seemed to need a husband to survive in today's society. And she really knew no one here. Well, hardly anyone. Perhaps she should return to Kansas City, but the idea of facing that trip again so soon was appalling. In time she would go.

Seated at the table with Rose at the Continental House, considering the menu blocked out on a chalkboard, it suddenly occurred to her that there was one kind of woman who never seemed to need a husband. A woman like Rose.

Embarrassed at the thought, she said shyly, "Don't you ever wish you'd gotten married? Don't you ever need a man?"

Rose laughed. "I need a man every whipstitch, but a husband, no."

"It just seems so unfair that women have so little chance of survival, here or in Kansas City, without a husband."

"Well, life didn't come with a guarantee that it would be fair, child. We all just do the best we can."

The words were spoken with such melancholy that Dessa decided not to press the issue. Had Rose lost her one and only love and been driven to a life of prostitution? How sad.

Later that night, she lay wide awake in bed, thinking over her decision to remain in Virginia City temporarily. And she thought of Ben and the way his crystal-blue gaze had regarded her so coolly after their lips had touched. As if he had not been affected at all. He had kissed the tips of her fingers. He had precipitated the incident. How dare he walk away afterward, as if it meant absolutely nothing? Was he only playing with her? And just before she fell asleep came the most important question. Was she only playing with him like she did those young hellions who pursued her in Kansas City's society? And if she was, she had a feeling Ben Poole, once aroused, would not be so easily deterred by a coquettish laugh and a door closed in his face.

The next morning Maggie brought in a breakfast tray and shook Dessa awake.

"Come on, honey, get up. It's almost ten o'clock. My goodness, everyone's asking about you. Are you feeling poorly this morning?"

Dessa rose to her elbows and peered across the dim room, blinking when Maggie swept wide the heavy drapes and let in brilliant sunshine. Did it never rain in this place?

"Who's…?" she snuffled, not yet quite awake.

Maggie held out a steaming china cup. "Here, this'll get you humming. I hear you went riding with Ben yesterday." Maggie drew up a chair, as if prepared to hear the whole story.

Dessa sipped at the aromatic coffee laced with thick cream. "My goodness, did he tell you that?"

"Well, no. He didn't. He's not talking at all, so I thought…I mean, Virgie saw you ride out and she said Ben looked like he'd been at the cream pitcher."

"Oh, she did?" Dessa squinted at Maggie through the steam of the coffee. "Does he still look that way this morning?"

Maggie grinned wickedly. "What'd he try? What'd you do?"

Dessa glared. She couldn't admit it was mostly the other way around, yet she didn't want Maggie to think the worst. "We didn't do anything but go riding. Oh, we had a race across the meadow and back. He won, but only by a nose."

"Oh, that sounds wonderful. Ben doesn't have much fun, you know. He's so serious all the time, like he never learned how to laugh. And I suppose he didn't, really." Maggie hesitated a moment and studied Dessa thoughtfully. "I'm glad you went with him."

Dessa was surprised. "I thought…I mean…do you love Ben?" She surprised herself more than Maggie with the question.

"Well, of course I do. But not like you mean. He…I…well, when I first met Ben, Rose sent him to me to, you know, to give him his first lesson in manhood, if you know what I mean."

Dessa had sat up and eased her feet off the side of the bed, and now she picked rapidly at the food on the tray so she wouldn't have to meet Maggie's honest gaze.

Maggie laughed. "Rose said later that she sent him to me because he was so innocent and tongue-tied with her, and couldn't keep his eyes off her bosom. She thought she knew just what would cure his hankering. But more than that, he needed someone to care what happened to him. And so we never did it again. I just couldn't, you see. He needed…well, he needed more for someone to be his friend, to take the place of the sister he'd lost, the mother he'd lost, the soul he'd lost. Neither one of us thought doing it together was right after that."

Dessa slanted a quick look at Maggie's sincere countenance. How very intuitive of her to see such yearning in another person. She wondered what kind of compassion it took to realize when someone was so deep in despair. Briefly she also wondered if Maggie was being completely truthful about her feelings for Ben.

Maggie smiled shyly and shrugged her pretty creamy shoulders. Her propensity to go around half nude no longer bothered Dessa. It was the way of this place, she supposed. And wasn't it odd that she had grown used to it so quickly? It was time she moved out of here and to a place of her own, before she started acting as loose as the women here. Immediately she was ashamed of such a thought, and realized that if she'd spoken it aloud, she would have owed someone an apology. Would she never learn to rein in her judgments?

She nibbled at a fluffy biscuit. "Maggie, I don't think you should count on me to improve Ben's naturally sour disposition. We don't really get along too well."

"Oh, well, maybe not," was all Maggie said, but Dessa could tell the other woman didn't believe her for one minute. There was nothing she could do about that.

Someone rapped on the door. Thinking it might be Ben, Dessa dived back for the safety of her bedclothes, but when the door swung open, it was Rose.

"Dessa, Cal Reimer brought this a few minutes ago. It's from Cluney & Brown in Kansas City. I thought you might want it right away. Maggie, there's a fella downstairs asking for you. I told him it was kind of early to do business, but he said it wasn't business. I'd suggest you get dressed before you go down. From the look of him, seeing you like that might be his undoing."

Maggie flew from the room, her expression a study in confusion, and Rose backed out and closed the door, leaving Dessa alone with the telegraph wire.

She read it quickly, then took her time going over the words again. Someone had made a very generous offer for her daddy's business. Mr. Cluney thought she should take it. Would she return to Kansas City to take care of the matter? And by the way, he added, additional funds had been transferred to the Virginia City bank for her convenience.

She sank down on the edge of her bed, holding the paper open on her knees. Stop. No. Yes. The words darted through her mind. Why didn't they just handle this? What did she know about Daddy's business? It was too much. Why didn't Andrew handle it for her? He'd worked for Daddy for several years and was supposed to be her intended. Why did they bother her?

Once again, she felt hollow and bewildered at being totally alone in this strange wilderness. Here she sat with nothing to wear but a black funeral dress, no place to live but a brothel, no friends but a madam and her girls, with a young heathen who might or might not be courting her, and some stuffy lawyer wanted her to come home and face an unknown cigar-smoking businessman and discuss something about which she hadn't the slightest knowledge.

Well, she wouldn't go. That's all, she simply wouldn't go. Andrew and Cluney could take care of it for her. She had money in the bank, and what she wanted to do was go shopping for some clothes and a decent pair of shoes, and then find a place to live. And then she would search for the strange man whose image had haunted her since his fleeting appearance at her parents' funeral. Those were the things she wanted to do and so that's what she was going to do.

She crumpled the wire into a loose ball and tossed it on the bedside table.

During her afternoon shopping spree she must have walked every inch of Wallace Street. She marveled at the brick and native stone buildings with their Gothic windows set deep in massive walls. The office of the Montana Post newspaper sported such windows as did the territorial capitol building housing the headquarters hastily moved there from Bannack back in the gold rush days. She learned quickly that natives referred to the town as simply Virginia, and they were proud of their somewhat bloody past.

One storekeeper hurried to point out that in Boot Hill, along with ordinary citizenry, five of Plummer's road agents were buried. Plummer, he explained, was the sheriff who split his time between Virginia and Bannack wreaking havoc with his infamous road gang and enforcing law to favor his own thievery. Five of his road agents were hanged, the man said, on January 14, 1864. Plummer was to swing later, with his wife beating at her breast and begging the vigilantes to spare her man.

One of the worst of the outlaws was Helm, the man confided in low tones, who it was known was a cannibal. He once shared a human leg with a half-starved Indian.

She covered her mouth and gagged, horrified and slightly nauseated by the story. She couldn't tell whether the twinkle in the stout storekeeper's eye meant he was having her on or he just enjoyed the effect of his tale.

Laden with packages, she returned to the Golden Sun just at dusk. The dressmaker had promised her several frocks by the end of the week, and she had bought two ready-mades, one suitable for riding. She would ask Rose if she could take out the gelding she had so enjoyed riding the previous Sunday. She also bought undergarments and shoes, and was surprised to find a few of the styles she had left behind in Kansas City displayed in the shops of this territorial town.

Ben was leaning against the bar when Dessa struggled through the swinging doors with her armload of packages. One tottered atop the stack, fell off, and hit the floor. A hairy fellow shuffled to her assistance, but Ben beat him to it.

"I'll get that," he said, and grabbed the package right from under the man's outstretched grubby hand. "Here, ma'am, let me help you." He managed to dislodge some of the bundles from her grasp without causing the rest to fall, and followed her up the stairs and right into her room, bold as could be.

She let the parcels tumble to the chaise lounge and turned to him. "Thank you, Mr. Poole. Just drop them there, if you don't mind."

He blinked and instead of letting go his load just stared at her. Why was she being so proper, so formal? What had gotten into her? He figured at best to get hollered at for coming into her room, at worst to have something pitched at his head, and here she was sweet as honey.

"Well, have you lost your tongue?" she asked, and dropped down on the twin chaise. "Oh, Lordy, I'm tired. What a chore, and it's not done yet. I never thought to find so many up-to-date fashions. And what a pretty town. I hadn't really looked at it before. A shame there are so many empty buildings."

"It's the gold," Ben finally said, feeling as if his tongue had been permanently stuck to the top of his mouth.

"Gold?"

"It's gone, mostly."

She nodded, wondering if that really explained anything,

and automatically reached up and unpinned the bun she'd managed to twist in her hair that morning. Long burnished locks tumbled down around her face.

He spoke her name under his breath and she looked up at him expectantly.

Under her soft gaze Ben forgot what he was going to say, and she sat there with her brows raised, waiting, making him feel totally foolish. He tried to imagine she was Maggie or even Rose, with whom he conversed easily, but it didn't work. She looked at him with rich green eyes sparkling away her recent sorrow, tilted her saucy chin and smiled, and he was lost. Speechless and lost. What a fool he was. The more he told himself to stay away from her, the more he couldn't seem to do so. And on top of that, now she insisted on being nice to him.

He cleared his throat and at last put down the packages. "Well, then...I'd better be going."

She waited until he was at the open doorway. "Ben?"

He stopped, shoulders hunched, but didn't turn.

"Thank you for the help."

It was all she said, and he found himself somewhat disappointed. He wanted to run away, but he wanted to stay and talk. He had hoped she'd say more, yet chastised himself for thinking as much. Who would want to talk to someone who couldn't or wouldn't talk back?

Dessa sat on the lounge listening to his boots thunk-thunking down the stairs. One way or another she would break that barrier of silence he so quickly constructed when he thought his privacy was being threatened. It had almost come down Sunday when he asked her to go riding, and downstairs just now he'd started in just fine and then clammed up. It was more than just shyness, she knew. Some of the things Maggie and Rose had told her explained his reticence. The more she thought about what he had endured during the war, the more she compared him to her brother Mitchell. Could they have met somewhere on a battlefield? Or, if not, surely they had both suffered incredibly during the dreadful battles in which thousands of men were butchered in only a matter of minutes.

She had never stopped trying to learn about the war, imagining Mitchell's involvement. Now she put Ben there, too. But he was only a child, not a grown man. No wonder he had problems dealing with ordinary day-to-day living. She grew more and more determined to break through the shell around Ben Poole. It might even help her deal with the loss of her brother when she herself was so young. This change of heart surprised her almost as much as her decision to remain in Virginia City for a while. Things were happening to her which she didn't understand. Maybe she was growing up.

Since her coming-out men had chased after her, pursued her with serious and not so serious intent. She was used to it and was frankly intrigued by one who turned tail when she slowed to be caught. Ben obviously didn't know any of the rules of the game, but that was okay. She could teach him.

Tomorrow she'd see about renting a small place to live. Perhaps for a month or so. Despite her desire to just forget all about Kansas City, she did realize that a decision must be made, and soon. She was responsible for Daddy's business and it wouldn't be long before the famed Montana winter snows began to fly. She'd never get out of the mountains and down to the railroad if she waited too long.

Eight

"You didn't touch that girl, did you?" Rose asked sternly of Ben. He had joined her for an early breakfast before pulling out on a two-day run for the Bannon Freight Company.

"Which one, Rosie?" he replied with a glint in his eye.

"You know which one, and don't pull that cute-little-fellow-in-short-pants act on me."

Ben chewed much longer than was necessary while he thought about the question. He knew Rose and Dessa were on friendly terms. What had Dessa told her about him, or had she bothered to mention him at all?

Rose pushed sternly. "Ben, I don't like the look of this."

"I kissed her hand a couple of times. She's a pretty girl."

"That's precisely what she is. A girl."

"Well, Rosie, if you think she can't take care of herself, you're mistaken."

Rose looked him over closely, the breadth and height, her eyes measuring with exaggeration the broad shoulders and long legs. "Don't be utterly ridiculous, Ben Poole. No woman her size would ever be a match for a man, even one smaller than you."

His eyes flared. "Well, dammit Rosie, I'm not going to attack her. You ought to know that."

"Maybe not, but you can be mighty persuasive and she's not experienced in the ways of men. If I hear you've taken advantage of her, Ben, I'll thrash you, see if I don't."

His anger cooled by a vision of Rose thrashing him, Ben laughed. "Now, there's a picture, sure enough, Rosie. Thrash me, indeed."

"I mean it." Rose set down her china cup and glared at the man she thought of as her son.

He shoved his empty plate away and stood. "I know you do, and so do I. I was just enjoying myself a little. She liked it and I didn't push. In fact, I sensed she was a bit put out when I didn't go any further. We were just having a little fun, Rosie. Hell, nothin' wrong with that."

She smiled up at him fondly. He was right, of course, and she was glad to see him enjoying something for a change, but she still couldn't help worrying about the impressionable Dessa, who took everything so to heart. She changed the subject. "By the way, the next time you get free, I wish you'd go over my books. They're all a mess again. Give them your magic touch."

"It's not magic, Rose, it's just pure horse sense. If you'd spend a few minutes every day writing down your figures, you wouldn't have so much trouble."

"Hogwash, Ben. You see things I don't even understand when you look at all that jumble of numbers. I'll swear I don't know where you got the knack, but I'm pleased you've got it."

"Just born in me, I reckon. Numbers make sense, even when nothing else does. There are rules and you can explain them." He wanted to add that unlike his own feelings, he could deal with the ink scratches in her books, but he didn't. "Wiley and me'll be back from Three Forks tomorrow afternoon. I'll come on by and fix you up."

"Thank you, Ben, and mind what I said about Dessa."

Ben grinned and crossed to the open door. "I tell you

what, Rosie. You quit worrying so much about everyone else and think about yourself a little. I been hearing some rumblings about the fine upstanding women in this town and what they'd like to do to you and your girls. You might ought to talk to Walter Moohn. Those ladies are serious. They could cause you plenty of trouble."

"One thing's for dang sure, Ramey over at the Busted Mule is plenty worried about what they can do to his business."

"Well, he's always had him a yellow streak where women are concerned. I swear if one looks at him cross-eyed he crumbles into a little ball."

"Well, all the same, Rose, I'd be careful if I were you."

Right after lunch Rose and Dessa located a small empty dwelling near the end of Main Street that appeared quite suitable for a temporary home for the younger woman. Through the murky windowpanes they could see that there were two rooms but no furnishings.

"I can order a divan and some tables for the parlor," Dessa said. "Then I'll need a bed and washstand and armoire."

Rose marveled at the lilt in the girl's voice. Perhaps this was a good idea after all, for it seemed to perk her up just having something to do.

"I would think Arliss could fix you up with a bed right away. He's a right handy carpenter. Then, if you wanted to go ahead and move in while you waited for the rest of your things, you could. I'd be glad to loan you a feather bed." She tilted her head and regarded the girl a moment.

"You know, out here a woman who owns two kettles, a cast-iron skillet, and a coffeepot considers herself well off."

Dessa grinned, not sure if Rose was teasing, then threw her arms around her friend and hugged her right there on the street. "Oh, a feather bed would be wonderful, and so will sleeping in my own home again. Oh, not that I don't appreciate your hospitality, Rose. But I feel like I'm putting someone out being there, even though you say not."

Rose frowned. "I worry, though, about a young girl like you living alone. Won't you be frightened? There are some mighty unsavory characters in Virginia, sad to say." She pursed her pretty red lips and thought about what Molly Blair had said concerning the Golden Sun and the girls there. It was all in how you looked at a thing, she supposed. But still she couldn't' see that she and her girls were doing harm to anyone. They didn't, after all, go out on the street and drag men in against their will. It wasn't quite the same.

"Don't be silly, Rose. Right here on this well-traveled street? The sheriff keeps a lookout and his deputies, too. If it will make you happy, I'll put that lock on at night." She indicated the cumbersome padlock fastened to a hasp on the outside of the entry door.

"Arliss can put one on the inside as well. I think that's a good idea. Well, if you're sure this is what you want, let's get over to the bank and find out how we go about renting this place for you," Rose said, and took Dessa's arm.

When Ben and Wiley Moss rode back into town the next afternoon, worn out and dusty from the round-trip freight run to Three Forks, they noticed bright curtains on the window of the old Kraft place at the edge of town. Kraft had been one of the first prospectors to hit gold out at Alder Gulch, and he had thrown up the two-room plank house for him and his partner, no doubt thinking it a mansion after camping on the banks of a creek so long. Others had soon followed suit until the dwellings and their privies out back looked like a scattering of giant play blocks tossed across the town by a careless child.

As the wagon drew abreast of the house, the door swung open and out stepped Dessa Fallon in a bright blue dress and bonnet looking as much at home as any young woman in town. She looked up at the rattling of their passage and spied Ben.

Her hand came up in greeting, and Ben silently raised the Winchester above his head.

Wiley eyed him out of the corner of his eye. "Wanta git off?"

"Nope," Ben answered, and lowered the rifle.

"What it was, I seen you two lookin' at each other and figgered you just might want to be saying more than howdy." Wiley popped the leather reins on the horses' rumps.

Ben didn't answer, but he couldn't help turning to watch Dessa walk up the street in the direction of the Continental. Going out to supper, no doubt. Well, she could afford such a highfalutin eating place. He had to settle for beans and cornbread at Doolan's, or at best Sunday fried chicken at the Montana House.

What was she doing at the Kraft place? Surely she hadn't moved in there. With that one, he wouldn't be too surprised at anything she did. He found himself hoping that she would still be at the restaurant when he got cleaned up. He'd saunter in just like he belonged and sit with her awhile, order a glass of iced tea or cup of coffee, casual as hell, and hope he could afford to pay for it. Maybe he could even think of something clever to say to make her laugh. She'd look up at him, her eyes would shine with mirth, and her pink lips would widen so those pretty white teeth could peek out. He had a powerful need to be in her company, and just thinking about sitting across the table from her made him shiver.

For a moment after he stepped through the door of the Continental twenty minutes later, Ben thought Dessa had already eaten and gone. Then he saw her sitting off in one corner. Despite the lamp on the table and the hanging chandelier, pools of darkness shadowed her features. All the same, he didn't need to see her face to know it was her.

It was going to be difficult to casually detour clear to the back of the restaurant and appear to accidentally spot her, but as it turned out, he didn't have to. Dessa looked up, saw him, and lifted her hand ever so slightly. He nodded, smiled, and made a beeline for her.

With an attempt at cool composure, she watched Ben approach. His hair was wet; he'd tried to slick it down with little luck. A few curls hung along the collar of his shirt and over his ears. She wanted to trail her fingers through the thick mass and was shocked at the unexpected desire. With delight, she noted that he had left his hat on the rack at the door, so he didn't make a habit of wearing it to the table like she'd suspected.

Resting her chin on folded hands, she glanced up with a deliberate coquettish flutter of her long lashes. She couldn't help but giggle, and said, "Won't you please join me, Mr. Poole?"

He pulled out the chair next to her. "I'd be most proud, Miss Fallon."

"I was hoping you'd come."

"Me, too," Ben said.

They both laughed.

Dessa sighed and lifted her napkin, then refolded it. "Well," she finally said.

"Yes. Uh, I saw you earlier. Coming out of the Kraft place. I thought it was empty...I mean, who were you visiting?"

"I wasn't visiting anyone. I rented it. I live there. Isn't that wonderful?"

"Alone?" He thought her youthful excitement quite refreshing, but he wasn't sure how he felt about her living alone.

"Now, don't you start on me, too. I had to convince Rose."

"No easy feat."

Laurie Sue came to their table to ask if Dessa wanted dessert and if Ben wanted anything. That forestalled any further discussion of Dessa's living arrangements for the moment.

They ordered blackberry cobbler and Ben asked for a large glass of milk, hoping he had enough money on him to pay for it.

Dessa watched him devour the large serving of cobbler and offered most of her own to him.

Take it, I'm so full," she said, and held up the dish, her spoon still sunk deep in the sugary purple crust.

He took the offered dessert and had the spoon in his mouth before he realized she had licked it. He held it between his lips too long, staring across the table at her and thinking of her small pink tongue lapping at the silver. Her gaze went from his lips clamped around the spoon to his gleaming eyes, and then she caught on, too.

He pulled the spoon free very slowly before licking it front to back and placing it in the dish. Gazing directly at her, he took a big drink of milk.

Dessa patted at her lips with the napkin. He was deliberately sending her a message, and she knew if she picked up on it, he would do just what he'd done when they went riding. Back off like a scared rabbit. She wasn't sure what kind of game this was, or if it was just his way, but she was determined to thwart him, one way or another, before the evening was over.

When they finished, Dessa waited for Ben to pull her chair back from the table, until she realized that he was up and gone, already headed across the room. He could do with some civilizing, but then she'd known that all along, hadn't she? And wasn't that one of the things that attracted her to him?

He stopped to pay his bill, and was shocked when the man handed him the tab for Dessa's meal as well. Amazed, Ben studied the figures. Three dollars and forty-nine cents for supper? Another two bits for his cobbler and milk? Hell, he could buy a whole supper down at Doolan's and wash it down with a beer for what his alone cost. Worse, he didn't have that much on him.

Dessa stood against his arm, peered over at the two slips he held in his hand, and took hers away from him.

"You didn't ask me to supper, Mr. Poole. I certainly don't expect you to pay for it," she said loudly enough for those nearby to hear.

She noticed that Ben's ears turned red, but he didn't protest. Probably didn't have any money, maybe not even enough to pay for his own.

"Give me yours, too," she whispered.

Ben pulled it away from her reach, mumbled low, "No, I can pay my own."

"No, it's okay. I'll pay it," she hissed.

"You will not," he said aloud.

Several of the diners turned their heads to stare, and the man waiting for them to pay glared hard at Ben.

"Stop being such a dolt," Dessa said.

"I am not a dolt." Ben tossed two coins on the tray the man held imperiously before him and slammed out of the restaurant.

His heels came down so hard on the boardwalk they could be heard all the way up the street to the Golden Sun. He jammed his hands down in the pockets of his britches to keep from flailing them around in the air above his head as he muttered to himself.

"I'll show her dolt. Blasted spoiled little imp. She needs a daddy to give her a good spanking, that's what she needs. Too bad she ain't got herself any folks to teach her how to behave."

He reached the Golden Sun and was almost past the doors when he remembered his promise to Rose about straightening out her usual financial mess.

"Ah, dang it all and hell's bells." He was in no mood to put up with another woman, even if it was Rose. All he wanted to do was ride out of town and sit on a damn rock and stare off into the night, so he just kept right on going.

A half-moon hung high in the sky, and as the sun crept behind the mountains to the west, its silvery light played peekaboo with the darkness. The elongated shadows cast by the buildings across the way looked like outsized tombstones shaped to fit all the men he had seen die in the war. Men who lay in mass graves, their bodies unclaimed. And striding along, he imagined the thunder of cannons, felt the solid jar of the earth up through the soles of his feet, and heard the eternal cry of that child he'd been.

Off in the distance a coyote set up a forlorn howl that fit Ben's mood like a coat. He definitely needed the soothing of a child's small hand in his. The softness of an innocent babe's cheek against his stubbled jaw would drive away the long and lingering memories. He'd ride out to see Sarah and the children, and everything else could just be damned. Rose and her books could just wait another day. She couldn't get them in much more of a mess than they already were.

He went down to the stable and asked for Beauty. Rose had left standing orders that he could have her anytime he pleased, and so no questions were asked. He saddled quickly, more anxious than ever to hold the babies in his arms and listen to Sarah's soft voice forgiving him once more.

Dessa had rushed away from the Continental as quickly as she could after Ben's rowdy exit. She didn't know what she'd expected of the rough frontiersman. Yet something deep inside her flared with compassion. He had been embarrassed and so reacted in the only way he knew. However, the scene went a long way toward convincing her that she and Ben Poole had nothing whatsoever in common. She just wished she could forget the touch of his warm lips on her hand, the way his frosty eyes thawed when she gazed into them, his heart beating under her cheek when he carried her in his arms—twice now—with such tenderness.

It was dark under the eaves of her new home when she arrived, and she had to work awhile to fit the key into the padlock. Arliss had left the original padlock on the outside of her door since the bank had given her the key, and merely installed a second hasp on the inside so she could lock herself in at night.

"Was a time nobody had to lock up," he explained, "but this town's got so wild, young woman like you has to be extra careful. All the riffraff and all. Wouldn't do to leave the latchstring out."

Dessa had instantly liked Arliss Long, a wind-burned and skinny old prospector who had hung up his pan and settled down to do odd jobs around town when the gold findings played out.

She was affixing the inside padlock when there was a rap on the door. At first she thought Ben must have followed her, but she dismissed that instantly. He had been much too embarrassed and angry, and was nowhere in sight by the time she exited the restaurant.

"Who is it, please?" She left the key inserted in the lock, waiting for a reply.

"Sheriff Moohn, Miss Fallon. I've got something for you."

Dessa unlocked the door and opened it. "If you'll wait just a moment, I'll light a lamp. It grew dark while I was gone."

"These little places are plumb gloomy inside all day long, what with those tiny little peepholes of windows. I expect folks who built them didn't want to pay for glass, or just couldn't be bothered, seeing as how they spent their whole entire days and much of their nights out on some rocky stream bed panning for gold."

While the laconic sheriff drifted inside and made conversation, Dessa found the lamp and matches just where she'd placed them on a wooden crate that served as a temporary table. She removed the globe and lit the wick. Once the flame was adjusted, she slipped the glass back on and turned to face Walter Moohn. He held a wrapped parcel in one hand, his hat in the other.

She gestured around the parlor. "I'm sorry I can't ask you to sit, but I have no furniture yet to speak of."

"Doesn't matter, ma'am. I'm plumb ashamed of myself for forgetting this, but in all the excitement and getting up the posse and everything, I forgot. This must have belonged to your folks, Miss Fallon. Like I said, I'm sorry I didn't get it to you before this time.

"I was rummaging around through the safe this evening and run across it. That's the first I've thought of it since the fire and the stage robbery and everything. I apologize, and hope it wasn't something you needed."

Dessa gazed at the parcel through his entire explanation, scarcely hearing his words. She recognized the brown paper wrapper, could tell right away it was taken from a roll like that commonly used to wrap purchases in mercantiles. It was tied with plain white twine.

"I'm not sure what it could be."

"Well, ma'am, I'm not, either. All I know is it was laying out a ways from the upstairs window of the mercantile, you know, like it had been tossed out there when they seen they couldn't..." He paused and licked his lips.

Dessa grew extremely conscious of the sound of his tongue on the parched flesh and the flutter of the flame in the lamp. She felt as if her heart had stopped beating. Outside, someone shouted and a horse galloped away, making her jump.

Everything in her mind said grab hold of the package, hold it to her breast, take in the feel of her mother's hands as she wrapped the thick paper, tied the wrinkled string. But she couldn't lift her hands, take the package, though Sheriff Moohn held it so that it was almost touching her.

Unable to reach out, she swayed and closed her eyes. Flames tried to swallow her up in their heat and fury, curling around her toes and licking upward. The heat, the pain. Oh, poor mother. Poor dear daddy. She couldn't bear thinking about it.

Gasping, she said, "I...I can't...I mean, thank you so much. Could you just...would you please just put it there on the table beside the lamp? I need...I want to..." To her astonishment, tears gushed and sadness overpowered her so that she almost collapsed to the floor.

Moohn grabbed her by one elbow and got rid of the parcel so he could support her. "Well, now, there, there. I didn't mean to upset you so. Can I get you anything? Could I go get Miss Rose for you?"

Dessa shook her head vehemently. It was time she stopped leaning on everyone else. She had to learn to handle this grief; she couldn't just continue to expect someone else to take care of her. The unexpected tears were maddening, but she couldn't make them stop.

"No, no, thank you," she managed. "I'll just retire for the night. Please, just go now."

"Are you sure?" The lanky sheriff gazed closely at her. "You're pale as a sheet. Just let me get Miss Rose."

"No," Dessa shouted. She held out her hands, as if to soothe the distressed sheriff. "I'm sorry, no. I'll be fine."

"Well, if you're sure. I'll just go, then. If you need anything, you just open this here door and holler, and one of my deputies will be right here, you hear me, now?"

She nodded, unable to utter another word past the raging sorrow boiling up in her throat. Why didn't he just go, leave her be? Let her throw herself on the bed and cry this away?

Finally he did, and she didn't bother to lock the door before stumbling into the next room and throwing herself facedown on the sweet-smelling feather bed Rose Langue had provided.

A half-moon hung on the lip of the mountains to the west when Ben rode back into Virginia City. The clop-clop of the mare's hooves echoed in the silent town. Down the way, lights glowed in the Golden Sun, and farther on, the Busted Mule showed signs of some activity. Otherwise the streets were as still as those of a ghost town.

A large bird soared overhead, flying so low Ben felt the air stir with its passing. An owl out on its nightly hunt. He reined in the mare to watch the black shadow swoop to the ground, then glide back into the sky. The bird's passage blotted out the light of the moon for a split second and Ben blinked. For no apparent reason he could think of, he felt the sting of tears. He never cried, yet here he was getting all wet-eyed. What nonsense.

Lord God, what a night. The air was as soft as down, yet he could sense, creeping in around the edges, the coming snows of winter in the mountains. Yet another winter that would find him with no home to speak of.

While he gawked around at the sky the mare had come to a halt right in the middle of the street, and he made a kissing sound to her. She started, as if he'd awakened her, and Ben chuckled despite himself.

'Your thoughts meandering, too, honey?" he asked, and headed her toward the livery stable.

When he passed Dessa's, he didn't slow but took note of a pale light still burning in the main room. She probably fell asleep and left the lamp turned on. What a waste, but he supposed she could afford to burn up all that coal oil for useless light.

After he left the mare at the livery, Ben walked back down to the Kraft place. To Dessa Fallon's place. He could no more have stopped himself than he could have followed in flight the owl he'd seen night hunting.

The door was off the latch. Foolish of her. Anyone could walk in. He grinned and eased it open, wincing when the boards creaked underfoot. If he awoke her, she'd be frightened, might even throw a lamp at him. Maybe could kill him outright, for all he knew. He paused in the doorway to the small bedroom and listened. Her breathing was wispy, but if he held his own breath, he could hear her inhale and exhale.

His heart pounded in his chest and he held the flat of one hand over it. Surely she'd hear. For a moment he closed his eyes and breathed deeply of her scent, thinking of an early morning, dew-frosted meadow. A taste filled his mouth, the golden sweet taste of her skin, and he crept through the soft glow of the lamp to the side of her bed.

In sleep she looked even younger than when she was awake. One hand lay palm open beside her cheek, and the thick dark hair spread all around her head. Long eyelashes touched the pale cheeks like a dense fringe.

He felt a painful urge to touch her, kiss her, hold her, like he'd done when he carried her into his life. Not knowing then that such a simple, effortless act could so interrupt his existence. Sucking in a breath, he bent and left a faint kiss on her forehead.

"Sleep well, Dessa Fallon, sleep well. I'll try not to mess up your life too much. If I can help it." He tiptoed silently away. "If I can help it," he repeated as he pulled the door closed and stepped out onto the boardwalk.

He only hesitated a moment before he snapped the outside hasp shut and fastened the lock through it. It would keep her safe, and she could get someone to open it for her come morning. He had to smile a little when he thought of how mad she would be when she awoke and found herself locked in. Of how she might even come looking for who would do such a thing.

She shouldn't be so careless, though, alone like she was. She just shouldn't be so damned careless.

Nine

The next morning Arliss came pounding on the door, waking Dessa. She had to throw her key out the slot of a window so he could open the lock. There was little time to wonder how the thing got fastened on the outside. By the time she had quickly dressed, Arliss and a young boy he called Thad had carried a three-drawer chest into her house, saying someone had ordered it, then didn't pick it up and it was just in his way. She insisted on paying him a fair price for the piece of furniture, and asked the men to place it in the smaller room. The dresser went well with the frame and headboard Arliss had fashioned of pine. With the borrowed feather ticking and bright patchwork quilts, the room took on a homey appearance.

As soon as he turned loose of his side of the dresser, Thad received a curt nod from the older man and raced out the front door. Down the street she heard the shouting of young voices and supposed he had gone back to his play. Children here on the frontier did little enough of that and she listened to their laughter with pleasure.

When she turned her attention back to Arliss, she saw he stood in the center of the small parlor, measuring the wall space with a length of cord, squinting his small brown eyes thoughtfully. He wore a leather apron that hung to his knees. Under it were the homespuns most frontiersmen wore, faded so that not much color remained.

"Could use a few pieces in this here space," he drawled, indicating with both hands the length of one wall. "Yonder, you'll have to put a stove ere you freeze come winter. See the pipe hole covered over there in the ceiling."

Dessa smiled secretly at his salesmanship. He would end up making every piece of furniture save the stove and divan. She didn't mind at all; he was a fine craftsman who never left rough or sharp edges and finished his work with flair. His talk about a stove moved her thoughts to the summons from Cluney & Brown to return to Kansas City. Perhaps she wouldn't be here to need a stove. Shaking her head over that unanswered question, she said, "I could use a table and chairs. I've ordered an upholstered divan."

Arliss grinned and revealed a gap center front where he was missing a tooth. "Case a young gendeman comes to call, you mean?"

Folks out here sure put themselves right into your life. She wondered if she would ever get used to their casual familiarity.

Arliss rubbed the calloused palms of both hands down the front of his leather apron, making a scraping sound. "Table and chairs it is. Got any preferences other than they be usable?"

Dessa smiled at him. "No, usable is just fine. Whatever works best." She didn't ask him how much they would cost.

"I reckon I could have them brought by in a week or ten days. Got some other pieces to put together. Women moving in means more work for me. Man, he's satisfied with a chair or two, maybe a bed, and he can knock together a plank table hisself that'll suit him just fine. But you women get turned loose in a house, and you want her right fancy. Oh, I ain't griping, mind. Good for my business." He raised his chin to catch her gaze.

"Made all the benches and desktops for the school, made the church pews." He laughed. "Funny, ain't it, how they'll build a school first, then a church? Women is right down funny, when you get to it."

"I reckon," Dessa said absently, then looked up at the man in surprise. Reckon? She was beginning to sound like these frontierspeople.

Arliss backed toward the door, which he'd left standing open, as was the custom when a man entered a single woman's room. "Lock working okay for ya?"

Dessa nodded. "Oh, yes, just fine. Thank you."

"I noted it was locked on the outside and was wondering if something is wrong with this one in here." Arliss tugged at the hasp.

"Uh, no. I don't know...I mean, I thought...Never mind, it was just a mix-up. Both are working fine."

Arliss squinted at her a few seconds, then nodded and backed out, pulling the door closed with a firm thud.

Who had locked her in last night, and why? She pondered that a few moments, then shrugged. Probably someone came along whom she knew and simply decided to lock up. It wasn't, after all, a dastardly deed, though it might have been bothersome had she not been able to get someone's attention right away. Dismissing the minor mystery, she whirled around in the pleasant room. She could imagine a warm fire in a potbellied stove, a floral print divan, maybe a fine sideboard over on the other wall. She could get one of those stoves that she could use both for heating and cooking. There was room for the table and chairs over there by the window near where she would put the sideboard. It would hold dishes and she could order a mirror to hang above it to reflect the room, and sunny yellow curtains to make the window look larger.

What was she thinking of? She was going back to Kansas City before the snow flew, wasn't she? This was only temporary, wasn't it?

In the bedroom, she began to fold her few articles of clothing into the chest of drawers. With trepidation she picked up the package the sheriff had delivered the night before. The wrapper crinkled under her fingers. It was just a package. Something her mother or father had thought valuable, perhaps. Or maybe it belonged to someone else. Someone who dropped it earlier and it just wasn't found until the fire. Not likely, though, she realized. No, this belonged to Mother, she was sure of it. She hugged it close for a moment, then placed it in the bottom drawer of the new chest.

Some evening she would open it, but not today. The day was too beautiful to be ruined by a fresh round of grief. After a night's sleep she was no closer to a decision as to what she would do. Go or stay. Go or stay. And what about Ben Poole? She really wanted to explore her feelings where he was concerned. And that was not easy to do, with him backing off at every turn. Maybe she could think of some way to get to know him better. Get him talking about himself and his dreams. There must be feelings fit to burst buried in a man like him. It wasn't a thing Dessa Fallon had ever had to do, woo a man. They had always come to her the minute she raised an eyebrow or crooked a finger. Ben came, sure enough, but then he ran away again. It was frustrating to be so attracted to him, only to have him flee before she could put a finger on what the attraction was.

Dismissing her wandering thoughts, she fetched her reticule from the bedroom and stepped outside into yet another glorious morning. Living in Missouri and on the banks of a river, she had grown used to long, wet days in September, fogs rising up off the water of an early morning. This dry mountain air was sweeter than a rose garden, cleaner than the streams that flowed down from the snowcapped peaks, and the indigo blue sky just spread out forever, bigger than anything she had ever in her life imagined. Montana Territory was indeed a marvelous place.

Gazing up into the morning sunlight, she turned a circle on the boardwalk and breathed deeply.

"A good morning to you, ma'am," a voice called, and she heard the familiar rattle of the freight wagon rumbling down the street.

Perched on the seat, Wiley Moss held two hands-ful of leather reins, so he couldn't wave, but she knew it was he who had called out. Ben sat on the other side of Wiley, and appeared not to even be looking her way.

She sang out, "A very good morning to you, Mr. Moss, and you, too, Mr. Ben Poole."

Ben actually lifted his hat and leaned out where he could see her, but he didn't say anything at all. Hands clasped in front of her, Dessa watched the wagon until it curved out of sight around a bend outside of town. Raising her shoulders in a silent question, she headed toward the Continental House for breakfast. She figured Rose would be there and they could visit awhile.

Rose patted the chair beside her when Dessa approached her table. "You look very well this morning, child. I believe you're finally on the mend. This mountain air will do it every time. Healing, that's what it is."

Dessa slipped into the chair and removed her gloves. "I'm in the mood for something special this morning."

"Perhaps a mushroom omelet. Or champagne with fruit. Have you ever drank champagne for breakfast?" Rose asked with a sly smile.

"Why, yes, I have. Do you think Kansas City is uncivilized? But don't tell me they have such cuisine here?" Dessa glanced around the room.

"Katrina serves only the best. Her chef is from Switzerland."

Dessa raised her brows, impressed. "Well, then, I do believe I'm in the mood for champagne and perhaps melon. If that's what you're having."

Rose guffawed. "Hate the stuff, myself. I'm having an omelet, so light and fluffy it may float off the plate when the waiter carries it in. But do have your champagne, dear."

Rose took a sip of coffee, eyed Dessa over the cup's rim. "By the way, I thought you might enjoy attending a concert at the Opera House Saturday."

"A concert?" Dessa's eyes widened. "Oh, yes, let's do."

"Fine. But I won't be going, I'm too busy on Saturday nights. I have arranged for Desmond Venable to accompany you. He's eligible and should be compatible. Not as rough around the edges as our Ben." Rose slanted a crafty look at Dessa.

What was she up to now? First she encouraged her to take up with Ben, now she was shoving her in another direction. Dessa didn't know what to make of the situation, but didn't want to miss the chance to enjoy a concert, whomever the escort.

So she agreed, and the matter was settled. Even as she popped the first bite-sized piece of golden melon into her mouth, Dessa couldn't help thinking of Ben Poole, riding out across the rough countryside in the dust and hot sun. Had he ever drank champagne for breakfast? For that matter, had he ever drank champagne at all, or attended a concert or a ball? Probably didn't even dance. Much as she had noticed his presence when she stayed at the Golden Sun, she'd never seen him dancing with the girls.

She didn't see Ben again until the night of the concert. She wore a new dress, crimson with tiny pale pink flowers and a full skirt. Mrs. Fabrini had done a marvelous job with the fit. The waist hugged her slim figure and the puffed sleeves were just the perfect length. Gloved hand tucked into the crooked elbow of Desmond Venable, she strode languidly along the boardwalk, feeling almost as if she were carefree once again.

Desmond was a pleasant enough young man with automatic manners that offered her no special deference. They were just something he had learned, just as he had learned to dress properly, comb his hair, and speak well, as befits the son of a banker. With her high-heeled button shoes she was nearly as tall as he, and his flesh felt soft under her hand. He was endowed with neither the strength nor the gentleness of Ben Poole, despite his good manners and perfect hygiene.

All the same, she was pleased to be stepping out with a young man. It made her feel as if life might perhaps continue despite the tragedy of her parents' death and all the confusion that had created.

Together the two threaded their way along the boardwalk. The streets were crowded, and concert-goers were easily discernible from men headed for a night at the Busted Mule or the Golden Sun.

Ben Poole was one of the latter, but he was fresh from the bathhouse and the new barbershop, a welcome addition to town. He spied Dessa immediately, for she stood out among the crowd like a gold nugget in a frothing creek bed. The berry color of her dress made her look good enough to eat, and he had a sudden appetite for just such an indulgence. She had piled her dark curls high atop her head and wore a feathered hat cocked to one side. Her green eyes flashed with excitement.

Ben stumbled over a riser on the walk while staring at her, then nearly tangled his feet together. She spotted him and said something to her companion, causing Ben to register the young man. So that kind of dandy was what she really preferred.

Then Dessa came toward him, holding out one hand. "Why, Ben Poole. How...how nice you look."

Ben shifted and gazed down at his boot tops. If she was trying to embarrass him, she was doing a good job.

"Ben, this is my...uh...my friend, Desmond Venable. Desmond, this is Ben Poole, the young man who saved my life."

Venable tipped his expensive gray bowler as if to call attention to the difference in it and Ben's sweat-stained hat. Ben noted the man had doused his short hair with macassar oil until it gleamed. Venable offered to shake hands. Ben ignored him to stare at Dessa, who stared right back.

She knew as soon as she looked up into Ben's face that she would rather be with him in the back of a wagon than walking down the street with her arm tucked inside Desmond's. She spotted the hurtful look that passed quickly over Ben's features. Maybe he did care about her. Just a little.

"You look beautiful, ma'am," he said, and, like he had done so many times before, lifted her gloved hand. Just as he bent to kiss it, he turned her arm ever so gently and placed his lips at the bare pulse point of her wrist. She felt the briefest flick of his warm tongue at the throbbing of her heart, a gesture that sent delightful shivers deep into her core.

She sucked in a quick breath and nibbled at her lower lip as he let go of her wrist. He might as well have kissed her on the mouth, the way the act affected her. When he raised his head, he kept her fingers in his own broad palm and cast a sensuous look at her from beneath a long sweep of black lashes. Tiny flecks of deep blue flashed in the ice of his eyes and he held her gaze so long she felt herself growing light-headed.

Then he smiled, released her hand, and placed his hat back on his head firmly. He appeared to be screwing it down to his head, as if in preparation for battle. "Pleasure to meet you, Venable," he said in a brief aside, and strode off, not once looking at the man he addressed.

"Ought to've knocked his cocked hat off his cocky head," Ben muttered as he swung through the crowd on the boardwalk and made his way to the bat-wing doors of the Golden Sun. "Like to see that sumbitch even pick her off her feet, let alone tote her across a room, should she need it."

"Well, hello, Ben," Rose said from behind the bar. "You look sour enough to clabber milk." She drew him a brew without asking and sloshed some out when she slid him the foamy glass.

"Who's that yahoo with Dessa out yonder?"

"Why, Ben. By your tone you'd think you really cared for the pretty little thing. Couldn't prove it by the way you've been acting toward her lately."

Ben studied Rose thoughtfully, eyes squinched almost shut. "Whose idea was it, hers or yours?"

Rose spread a scarlet-nailed hand across her bare bosom. "Me? Whatever are you talking about?"

"I'm plumb ashamed of you. Didn't I do your books? Didn't I help you straighten out that mess before you got it so scrambled it'd took a act of God? Didn't I? And now you go playing games with me, like I'm some stupid kid."

Rose laughed with obvious delight and changed the subject. "Have you talked to Maggie lately? Seems she's got herself a feller. An honest-to-goodness admirer. I think you should speak to her. He's trying to get her to marry him, go to California. The girl is all aflutter."

"Marry? Maggie? Don't be ridiculous, Rose." He tipped the glass and polished off more than half the cold beer, still thinking of the way Dessa laid her hand on that dandy's arm. "Well, Rose, I'm not falling for your tricks, nor Dessa's, either."

He gulped down the rest of the beer and wiped the foam off his mouth with the sleeve of his shirt. "Where's Virgie? I wanta see Virgie."

"Now, Ben," Rose warned. "Don't go doing nothing you'll regret."

Ben didn't say anything, just threw her a disgusted look.

A tall, long-legged redhead rose from a table near the dance floor and made her way toward him through the jostling Saturday night crowd. A tubby little man ran along behind, hollering, "Hey, I got the next dance. I done give you my token. Come on, gal."

Virgie ignored him and tucked herself up under Ben's arm. "Whatcha need, honey?"

Ben's resolve faded. What he needed wasn't Virgie. It wasn't even a massage under her expert hands. He gave her a quick hug. "Never mind, Virgie. I got somewhere to be. You go on and dance with the champ there. He needs you lots worse than I do."

Outside he glanced up and down the street. The concert goers had all settled into the opera house for their night of entertainment. Strands of music wafted through the streets, a sweet lyrical sound that tugged at his lonely heart.

"I hope she has a real good time with that no-account," he grumbled. "Serve her right if he proves to be as dumb as he looks. Just serve her right."

He scuffed off down the street, headed for the Busted Mule, where he could get in a good, cheap poker game at the back table that Ramey reserved for men like him.

Desmond fumbled with Dessa's key, finally getting it into the lock on her front door. She didn't open the door, but backed up against it, effectively barring his way inside if he had such a thing in mind.

He took her hand and kissed it. Nothing. Just a dry, polite touch of mouth to glove.

"The concert was lovely, Desmond."

"Yes, wasn't it? Liszt is a marvelously talented composer."

'Yes, but I prefer Chopin," she replied, though this night she actually had welcomed the fiery Liszt production performed quite adequately by the traveling orchestra. Chopin could be much too serene and lovelorn, which would only serve to depress her even more. Why couldn't she get Ben Poole off her mind?

"Well, perhaps next week? I see there will be a three-act play by Victor Hugo. I hear he's making quite a splash on the East Coast."

"Mmm. Perhaps. I'm really very tired now. Thank you again, Desmond."

She backed into the room and eased the door shut on something he was trying to say.

She had unfastened the bodice of her dress and slipped her arms out of the sleeves when someone tapped softly on the door. Desmond, coming back for something? She didn't think so. Who, then? The door rattled, and too late she realized she hadn't remembered to fasten the inside padlock.

"Dessa? It's okay, it's just me," a soft and very familiar voice said.

Before she could take any action, Ben stepped into the open doorway between the parlor and her bedroom. And there she stood in her camisole shift, the bodice of her dress draped down around her hips.

"Ben Poole, have you no manners at all? Walking into my house like this. Get out of here! What do you want?" She gestured with both hands. "No, don't answer that, just take yourself on out of here."

"Girl, you got to learn to lock that door," he said before actually catching sight of her. "My God, Dessa, you're so beautiful." He just stood there, the door ajar behind him, unable to take his eyes off her.

"Ben," she scolded loudly. "Out. Out, or I'll call someone."

He took off his hat and held it in both hands in front of him. "No, don't do that, Dessa. Don't call anyone. I'm going."

But he didn't go; he just remained right where he was, rooted to the spot, and so, for a beat or two, did she.

"You know I won't hurt you," he said, just above a whisper.

Oh, yes, you will, Ben Poole. But not in the way he meant at all. She trembled all over just watching him watching her. There was a longing in his features that she had never before seen on any man's countenance. It gave her goose bumps to realize he could want her with such fervor.

He broke the long silence. "I was just going home...and I was worried you forgot to lock your door again...I mean, I thought...I thought we could maybe talk, since you were still up and everything."

She nodded dumbly. So it was him who had locked her door. And what if he had come in first, watched her sleep? Shaking her head, she took a step toward him and the dress slid down around her hips.

Dear Lord, was she mesmerized?

She bunched the fabric up in both fists. "Wait in the parlor, then, I'll be right in."

He nodded and smiled. "Yes, yes. I'll just wait in the...the other room. You'll be right in."

He felt like a perfect fool as he sat on one of the two straight-backed wooden chairs in the otherwise empty room. It was a wonder she hadn't thrown something at him, barging in like this. But he couldn't help it. He no more could have walked past her place when he saw her shadow through the window then he could have flown up to the moon. He toyed nervously with his hat for a minute, then tossed it on the floor beside the chair and clenched his big hands together in his lap.

He ought to just jump and run, but all he could think of were the few times he'd been with this woman and how good it made him feel just to be in her presence. Even when she was annoying the thunder out of him, he enjoyed it. He couldn't forget how his three sisters were killed, slaughtered in their own home by faceless bushwhackers, and him away so he could do nothing but want to die himself when he found their lifeless bodies. Before he himself took to killing in the war. He had enjoyed that killing because it allowed him to vent his hate for the men who had slaughtered his family. Now all he wanted was peace, and Dessa gave him a peaceful feeling. Even Sarah's forgiveness couldn't grant him such serenity. He didn't know why, couldn't put his finger exactly on what Dessa did that was so different. There was a nagging something, though, in the far reaches of his mind, that told him he never could possess this woman. Not wholly or completely, and he was a fool to think otherwise.

She came back through the door, the dress on and properly buttoned up. She had removed the hat and in doing so loosened some of the curls so that they lay over one shoulder.

He rose and met her halfway. He'd never had the nerve to touch her except to hold her hand or arm, but now he extended his fingers to the curve of her cheek, where tendrils of hair hovered. Lamplight turned the curls auburn.

She looked up at him and ran the tip of her tongue over her upper lip so that it gleamed wetly.

Hungrily, he lowered his head and tasted that lip, and it was as if a hand took hold of his heart and squeezed. A small growling sound erupted from deep in his being.

Dessa gasped and leaned into his open mouth.

They stood that way for a moment, hands reaching for but not touching each other, lips and tongues exploring slowly, exquisitely.

Warmth and light poured through Dessa. The velvet, sweet-tasting softness of his mouth offered her succor of a kind she'd never expected. It was like drinking at the well of life, and she wanted it never to end. She stepped closer, not disturbing the kiss, but making herself comfortable against his thighs, his hard flat stomach, his quivering chest muscles.

He circled her waist with both arms, then snaked one hand up to cup her head.

Flashes of light burst behind her closed lids, and she felt herself losing all control. Her muscles tingled, as if overused and ready to collapse. Her breasts ached, her thighs trembled, and both legs went out from under her.

He caught her, deftly swept her up into his arms, and carried her to the bed, lying her there and kneeling beside her.

"Dessa, oh, God, Dessa. I want you. You're so beautiful."

He gave her another long, lingering wet kiss, to which she submitted totally. "But if I did this, Rose would have my hide nailed to a barn door. My dear sweet Dessa, I'll never hurt you. Never." He pulled back, took his hands away.

Her eyes were smoky with desire, her lips swollen; red spots flared on her cheeks, and he turned away to keep from throwing himself on her right there, hitching up the dress, and doing what they both wanted so desperately.

He sat with his back to her, gathering his strength.

"Ben?"

"Yes." Gruffly spoken.

"I've never felt like this."

"Nor me."

"Then don't turn away. You always run away"

"I want you so bad it hurts. I never wanted anyone like I want you."

She didn't believe that entirely. There were the women at the Golden Sun anytime he asked: He was their darling, and would never have to want for anything, much less the loving arms of a woman. But right at this moment it didn't matter. He was a man, and men had their needs, separate from women. But Lord, if his desire was more than hers at this moment, she certainly sympathized. Wondered how he was keeping any control. He was right, of course. They couldn't do what they wanted to do. It might be fine for girls like Maggie and Virgie, but not for her. If she let him soil her, then he would no longer want her, nor would any other man.

"Ben?"

Another gruff reply. 'Yes, oh God."

"Are you angry with me?"

"Lord, no. What about you?"

"Me?"

"Don't be mad at me, either, Dessa. I tried to stay away from you, I promise I did. I know what I am, what I've done. I know a woman like you can't possibly...I mean, you will want to marry someone like Desmond Venable, or his like. Or someone back in Kansas City. Not a man who sleeps on the ground under a damned old wagon, a man who owes more than he can ever pay.

"I can't build us a life, and I can't ask you for anything, Dessa. And I'll try not to let this happen again, I promise."

He rose quickly, angry now, but only at himself. "Why don't you just go on back to Kansas City, Dessa Fallon? Go on back and marry you some rich man who can give you what you deserve. You don't need some ragtag like me. You surely don't."

He was out of the room and gone before she could form a reply, or even cry out his name, which she did after he slammed the door. Over and over, lying there fully dressed in her bed, still warm in the place where he had sat, she called his name.

Ten

Maggie sang as she tripped down the stairs at the Golden Sun. "The man who drinks the red, red wine will never be a beau of mine. The man who is a whiskey sop will never hear my corset pop."

"While the song didn't exactly reflect her sentiments—Maggie didn't mind a nip or two of whiskey herself—she thought it a catchy tune and was amused by the lyrics.

She wondered if Samuel would be in tonight, almost hoped he wouldn't. It was better if he didn't see her doing her job. Then he'd just start in on her again to let him take her away from all this, and she was afraid to allow her life to be in the control of a man's whim. But Lord a'mighty, he had the most beautiful eyes and the sweetest touch. Rose was no help at all, being such a romantic. She believed a woman should grab what she could get whenever she could get it.

Rose was pleased to see the girl so happy, but she wasn't fond of Maggie's little song. It reminded her too much of that bunch of teetotalers running with Molly Blair.

Ever since the gold strikes in California in '49, a small contingency of women had been crusading against liquor. To think that their influence had finally erupted in Virginia City was upsetting. Such a movement could mean the end of Rose's business. The dour preacher's wife had managed to gather a retine of followers who were, if nothing else, annoying to the owner of a dance hall that also supplied doves and plenty of hard liquor to the needy of the male population.

This particular Saturday, a week after Ben's unfortunate experience with Dessa that had thrown him into a most foul mood, something he, refused to talk much about, Rose shifted her attention from Maggie to Sheriff Moohn, who slouched at one of the tables near the front door. She wondered where he stood on the issue between her and Molly Blair.

The dying sun threw long bars of fading gold across the plank floor. Moohn lazily kept an eye on what he could see of a street that teemed with humanity, as it had every Saturday in his memory. Since the stagecoach robbery and double killing, Rose had noticed that the sheriff appeared to expect trouble at any moment. She understood his reluctance to ride into Alder Gulch.

Only a few minutes later the group of women Rose had taken to calling the unholy brigade approached the Golden Sun from the north. They had obviously gathered at the church, planned their strategy, and set out, for their shouts preceded them along the length of Walker Street, causing quite a stir among the evening strollers.

Molly Blair led the pack. On one side strode the uncommonly stout Mrs. Johannsen, the druggist's wife, on the other, Miss Lorraine Twigg, the spinster sister of hotel owner Morris Twigg. The formidable front line brought the sheriff to his feet and outside in order to get a better look. Sensing more trouble than just a lot of noise, Rose followed him.

There were at least a dozen ladies sweeping along behind the three leaders. All carried exceedingly stern expressions. Each possessed a weapon: among them several garden hoes, a manure shovel or two, and more than a few straw brooms.

The ladies' long skirts stirred up a cloud of dust that hovered around them on this windless, and up to that moment peaceful, evening. The brigade fetched up in a seething clot outside the swinging batwing doors of the Golden Sun Saloon. Rose Langue was not surprised to be their chosen target.

Down at the far end of the street Dessa lounged comfortably on her brand-new divan delivered by a Bannon freighter—thankfully not by Wiley and Ben, whom she hadn't set eyes on since he left her bedroom the week before. The uproar outside interrupted her intent concentration on a pillow cover she was cross-stitching. She lay it aside to go to the window. Spotting the rowdy gathering at the Golden Sun, she forgot all about her needlework. What in the world was going on?

Hurrying outside, she lifted her skirts and ran in that direction. Soon she could make out a babble of harsh voices, but the women hadn't really developed any timing in their chants, so it was hard to understand their message.

She joined a growing crowd of onlookers. No one wanted to miss this. It might be more exciting than the three-act play about to begin at the opera house, in which it was rumored that the word breast would actually be spoken aloud on the stage.

Up on the boardwalk in front of the saloon, Sheriff Moohn and Rose bodily barred the door to the Golden Sun. At their backs clustered several of the girls, among them Maggie and a tall redheaded woman who shouted horrendous obscenities over Rose's shoulder. Several men in the crowd guffawed loudly and egged on both sides.

"You tell 'em, Virgie," one shouted, and spat a long stream of tobacco juice. It barely missed the boot of a man next to him, who gave him a shove.

Dessa studied the redhead. So that was the mysterious Virgie. The one Ben went to for back rubs, and that was all, or so he said.

She glanced around and spied a large man with gleaming blond hair running toward the gathering crowd. Ben Poole.

Her heart lurched. She had succeeded in avoiding even the sight of him all week long, ever since he had kissed her and carried her into her bedroom, only to stalk out of her house. She told herself she didn't want to see him now, but what she really meant, and she knew it, was that she feared her own feelings around him.

She edged her way deeper into the mass of onlookers just as someone screamed. Craning her neck, Dessa saw that Molly Blair had thrown herself up against Sheriff Moohn and was shaking her fist at the scantily clad women in the doorway behind him.

"Babylon whores," Molly cried, and took a swing over his shoulder with her broom, barely missing her target and Moohn's jaw.

Maggie knocked Moohn aside and lit on Molly Blair with both fists swinging. She locked her fingers in Molly's tightly pinned bun of hair, and the two women toppled to the boardwalk, where they rolled around.

"Bite 'er, Maggie girl. You got good teeth. Ain't you sunk 'em in me often enough? Bite 'er, I say." The bowlegged man doing the hollering jumped up and down and swung a dusty hat over his head. It caught the fellow next to him across the back of his neck.

"You danged idjit," the fellow shouted, and shoved his energetic neighbor, who stumbled backward into one of the unholy brigade, who in turn took a mighty swing at his backside with her manure shovel. It made a satisfying thunk.

Meanwhile, Maggie and Molly had rolled off the boardwalk and into the dusty street, where they continued to do very little damage to each other while they tumbled and kicked, locked together making noises like two bear cubs.

Dessa shoved through the excited crowd to get a front-row spot. Just as she emerged from between the sawing elbows of the barrel-chested blacksmith and a potbellied man she'd never seen before, the redheaded woman called Virgie literally exploded from the saloon. She wore even less clothing than Maggie, having removed her long stockings and whatever she might have worn over a black corset that didn't even entirely cover her breasts. At least Maggie had on pantaloons and shoes and stockings, too. Dessa shuddered to think what Virgie had been doing before all this started.

More concerned with fighting than covering up, Virgie launched herself into the unholy brigade, half of whom were swinging their odd assortment of weapons, while the other half crawled around in the dirt.

Behind Dessa someone stumbled and shoved her forward so that Virgie lit astraddle her back. Dessa went down, taking with her the spinster lady, Miss Twigg, who immediately lost what dignity she had left when she landed spraddle-legged with her dress up around her hips. Long legs kicking air, Virgie scrambled over Dessa and pounded poor Miss Twigg's head into the dusty street. One of the unholy brigade started whopping Virgie and Dessa with her broom in a very unladylike fashion. Dessa scrambled from the fray and headed for the safety of the boardwalk. Someone grabbed her by one leg and dragged her back into the tussle. She kicked out and caught solid bone, bringing forth a grunt.

From the sidelines large hands grabbed both her wrists and began to haul her in the other direction, so that she felt as if she were being pulled apart like a wishbone. The one holding her leg fell away, taking her shoe with him, and she and her would-be rescuer thudded up against the front wall of the Golden Sun.

By this time Dessa's hair hung over her face, so she had no idea whose stomach it was buried in. Whoever it was had hold of her upper arms and was trying to right her. She sputtered and struggled.

Behind her she heard Walter Moohn bellow, "Hold on. Ever one of you, hold on or I'll shoot."

No one paid him the least attention.

"Well, dang it, then, we'll just see," he shouted, and fired two quick shots.

From somewhere on the other end of town came answering gunfire, and those who had temporarily frozen at the first blast erupted into action again.

Dessa rolled around until she was sitting, and shoved the thick veil of hair away in time to see men flow out of the Busted Mule down the street, firing their guns into the air like they were being attacked by buzzards or the like.

Moohn holstered his gun, threw his hands straight up, and waded in among the brawling women, ignoring everyone else. He got a firm hold on Miss Twigg's arm and dragged her, along with Molly Blair, off down the street toward the jail.

Molly waved one hand high and shouted, "We'll clean up this sinful Babylon if it's the last thing we do. Whores. Whores. God will smite you down. We'll make this a decent place to raise our children, see if we don't," or words to that effect.

Rose, who had remained well back from the commotion, staggered outside laughing so hard she almost busted out of her corset. This was probably the best Saturday night she'd seen since the night the town received word that the war had ended. After the fracas was all over, she'd wager she would sell more whiskey and dance tokens than ever before. She didn't notice for quite some time the couple sprawled side by side on the boardwalk, propped up against the Golden Sun.

Dessa decided Rose had temporarily lost her mind and turned to her companion, whom she hadn't yet identified.

"You hurt?" he asked, eyes twinkling with mirth. She didn't look hurt, did she?

"Ben?"

He grinned sheepishly. "Dessa."

"Ben."

He laughed. "Dessa?"

"This is silly."

"Sure is. Did you ever see anything like it? I wonder if it'll be in the Post tomorrow."

"What were they doing? My goodness, wasn't that the preacher's wife?"

"Yeah, and the sister of our illustrious Morris Twigg, and Van Cleve's wife and daughter both. Fine upstanding ladies, one and all. Didn't see Dimsdale anywhere, did you?"

"The editor of the Post? I don't suppose I know him on sight. Look at that, my new dress is ripped." Dessa held out one arm where the sleeve was torn halfway up the inner seam.

Ben cupped her chin in his palm, licked his thumb, and wiped a smudge from her cheek. "You sure you're not hurt anywhere?" He ran his hands down over her shoulders and arms, then encircled her waist, rising to his knees.

She lifted her head to look up at him. That's when she saw a fine thread of blood trickling from the corner of his mouth and a darkening bruise there. "I'm not, but you are. You're bleeding, Ben." With trembling fingers she touched the bruise.

His eyes grew dark with longing, like pools of woodland water, and he lifted her so they were both on their feet and standing close together. Whatever decisions he'd made about this woman, he was a sucker for compassion, and when anyone fussed over him, the orphan in him embraced the gesture gratefully.

With very little effort on his part, she was in his arms, locked up against his sweat-stained and dusty shirt. Palm flat against her back, he felt perspiration dampening the fabric of her shirtwaist.

She took a deep, deep breath and held on to the breadth of this man who always seemed to present himself as a somewhat reluctant but solid fortress at her beck and call. What in the world was she going to do about the way she felt when he did that? It would be easier to figure out, if he wasn't forever running away. Perhaps that's what she should do, too.

Run away. Go back to Kansas City and marry Andrew.

"Hey," he whispered in her ear.

"Mmm?"

"Let me take you home."

She nodded against his chest, then let him take her hand and together they started to walk past the door of the Golden Sun. They didn't make it.

"Ben, Dessa. Come in, have a drink," Rose called out when she saw them strolling side by side, gazing at each other so intently they'd probably fall off the end of the boardwalk if someone didn't wake them up.

"Want to?" Ben whispered.

Dessa glanced inside, saw Rose sitting at a table. "I'm an awful mess."

"Aw, Rose don't care," Ben said. "Come on, a good fight deserves a cold brew."

She let Ben lead her inside. He surprised her by pulling out a chair like a perfect gentlemen and seating her in it.

"My land, you two look like you were caught up in the fray."

Ben threw one leg over the back of his chair and sat down with a rueful laugh. "Dessa here was right in the middle of it. All I did was try to rescue her."

She punched at him lightly. "Oh, sure, Ben Poole. Rescue me, indeed. You like to pulled me in two pieces out there. And I was pushed. You wouldn't know anything about that, would you?"

He spread one hand flat on his chest and widened his eyes. "Not me. I only rescue damsels in distress, I don't push them around. Isn't that right, Rosie?"

"If it isn't, it damn well better be," Rose teased.

At that moment Grisham brought over three brimming glasses of golden brew. While Dessa had been guilty of trying a nip or two of brandy on occasion, she had never tasted beer. With a throat as parched as sand, she decided now would be as good a time as any. She lifted the beaded mug to her mouth, tipped it gingerly, and took a sip. The froth tickled along her upper lip. She swallowed and shuddered, screwing up her face.

Ben and Rose both laughed.

"Don't waste it if you don't like it," Ben chided. He pulled a bandanna from his pocket and blotted at her mouth.

"Let the poor child alone," Rose said. "It's an acquired taste, dear," she told Dessa. "Maybe you'd like some root beer or sarsparilla instead."

Dessa took another swallow of the beer, eyes locked on Ben. Worse.

Maybe it tasted better when one simply drank it right down, all at once and fast. It was like medicine. And everyone knew you had to gulp that right on down and get it over with. So that's what she did with her mug of beer.

With the final swallow tears burst from her eyes and she gasped several times.

"How was it?" Ben asked.

"G-g-g...awful," she sputtered. "Just awful. Why do you drink it, anyway? Why would anyone even want to acquire a taste for something so foul?"

Ben laughed and Rose watched him like a proud mother.

When he touched the corner of his mouth and winced, Rose asked, "Does it hurt?"

"Nah, I was just surprised. I don't remember being hit."

"Maybe someone hit you with her broom," Dessa said, her tongue and lips feeling numb. For no apparent reason, she giggled, then burped. Hand over her mouth, she glared at Ben, then Rose.

"I think you'd better take Dessa home, Ben. She seems to be a bit tipsy."

Ben rose obediently.

"Do you always do whatever Rose tells you to?" Dessa asked, and gave him a coquettish glance from under her lashes. "I don't want to go home. I want to hear what happened to all those women. I am most certainly not pipsy."

Rose smothered a laugh. "Walter put them in jail."

At the same time, Ben said, "You may not be 'pipsy,' but I always mind my elders. Let's get you home."

Rose slapped the back of his hand, which was spread on the table.

Dessa ignored the play and tried to stick to the conversation. "Really? The preacher's wife in jail? Oh, my, isn't that diriculous?"

Rose and Ben burst out laughing.

"What? What did I say?"

Ben stood. "Diriculous? You're right, Rose. Dessa is drunk."

"Am not," Dessa said, and came to her feet. She swayed, put one hand to her forehead, and Ben reacted just in time to catch her before she slumped to the floor.

With her in his arms, he grinned down at Rose. "This is getting to be a habit."

"She's a sweet little thing, Ben. You behave yourself with her."

"Dammit, Rose. I told you before, I won't hurt her." He looked down at the peaceful, dirt-smeared face resting up against his chest. "I would never hurt her," he said softly.

After he left with his light burden, Rose sat at the table for a long while, thoughtfully sipping at her drink. Sometimes Ben had no notion what would hurt a woman, but she hoped he was right and he would never hurt Dessa Fallon, for Rose had grown extraordinarily fond of the courageous young woman. She wanted only the best for her. Loving Ben might be just that, but then again, it might not.

Meanwhile, Rose had her own problems. She saw the trouble tonight with the unholy brigade as only the beginning, for when something like this got started in a town, there was usually no way of shutting it down. Those churchgoing women would keep at her till they drove her out of Virginia City, of that she was sure. Then where would she go and what would she do?

Ben gently lay Dessa on her bed. He bent to remove her shoes, only to find she was missing one. He pulled the other off and massaged her feet, taking them both gently in his large hands.

She moaned softly and he let go, rose, and sat beside her. For a long while he simply gazed down upon her sleeping face. There lay the one thing he'd ever found that he wanted with all his heart and soul. It was a strange feeling for Ben, who had learned early not to attach himself to much of anything, especially if it was valuable. It just made the losing of it more painful.

At long last he bent forward and kissed her, first on the forehead, then on each cheek.

"Oh, you sweet one," he murmured, feeling a constriction around his heart. What he wouldn't give to hold her, to make love to her, to feel her respond in kind.

With the tips of his fingers, he brushed a lock of hair back from her face. This was exactly what he had been afraid would happen, the first time he ever laid eyes on her. And now look at him. It was already too late for caution. He would never recover from losing her, he was sure. And he was also just as sure that he could never hope to have her.

She was attracted to him, that he could see, but it was a game with her. A game she'd played all too often, he'd wager, leaving broken hearts lying about her like stones in a creek. How could he think she might choose him? A woman like her, used to the finest. At the moment, she was enjoying playing her cat-and-mouse game with him because she was temporarily cast adrift, but once she got her wits about her, recovered from her grief, and returned to her home, she'd forget Ben Poole ever existed. It was just as well, too, considering the things he'd done. He had no business with a good woman, seeing as how he'd already ruined the life of one.

With tenderness he pulled the quilt up and tucked it firmly under her chin.

Studying her features as if he could memorize them for all time, he faced the truth. Dessa Fallon had left her mark on him, and it would be there forever, like a brand or a scar. For as long as he lived he would see her face every time he closed his eyes, even if he never saw her again.

Soon after Ben and Dessa left, Moohn joined Rose, declaring that his jail was fit to burst at the seams. "One cell's overflowing with yahoos, the other with some fine women who are downright plagued with me at the moment," he told her.

"How'd you manage that?"

"Once I got the attention of some of my deputies, who were out there in the midst of things themselves, it wasn't too hard to round up the ladies. The men took a bit longer. A conk or two on some heads worked wonders."

"You going to keep 'em the night?"

Moohn chuckled and shook his head. "I roused as many husbands as could be found to come down and rescue their women. Miss Twigg's brother was fit to be tied. He'll keep her locked up a week. I'll let the rest go at dawn. Sleeping on a hard floor won't do any of them too much harm."

"Walter, those women will never forgive you for this. They see me as the lawbreaker."

Moohn gazed balefully at the table. "I know, Rose. I know. But they disturbed the peace. It'd been you, I'd a done the same. Sorry about Maggie and Virgie, but they was in it tooth and toenail, too."

Rose took his sun-wrinkled hand. "I know. They'll sleep it off and forgive you. You're a good and honest man, Walter Moohn. But sooner or later, you're going to have to come down on the other side in this issue, mark my words."

Walter sighed. 'You read the Post the other day? That letter from the feller trying to stir up more trouble. Could be what set off this particular uprising."

"I didn't read it," Rose said absently. What harm could a letter in a newspaper do?

"He wrote that it was time we pitched into that nuisance called by some, a dance house. Reckon that's your place, Miss Rose. He suggested that the license fee you pay is what makes the law excuse your misdeeds. Said something about drunken prostitutes and their partners making so much noise he can't sleep."

Rose drew herself up. "My girls don't fornicate in the streets, nor do they stagger around drunk."

Walter patted at her arm. "I know, I know."

"So what else? Did Dimsdale remark on it?"

"Oh, he'd already had his say a few months back when he begged the good Lord to deliver him from bluestockings, bloomers, and strong-minded she-males generally. But this feller what wrote the letter said he and his neighbors would be more than proud to make up the difference to the city what they'd lose if the dance house was closed down."

"Four hundred dollars? He's willing to come up with that to shut me down?" Rose was aghast. "And every year thereafter? This is plumb foolish, Walter. I'm not hurting anyone."

"I wouldn't worry too much about it. You know they ain't no law agin this place, Rose. And till they is, well, they're all just blowing in the wind."

"But they elect you to office, and they'll soon outweigh those who want to keep these saloons. The law can be changed. It'll be a fair town one of these days."

Moohn squeezed her fingers. "Yeah, folks want to come out here to find what they're looking for, a wildness and newness. And they bring their society plunder with 'em, so they're right back where they started 'fore they come here."

"Hell, Rose, let's you and me just up and move on. We could find someplace that's like this place used to be."

Rose pulled her hand away gently. "You and me, Walter?"

He nodded and pinned her with a squinty stare. "You and me, Rose. Oh, I know you loved that Englishman...and I know what kind of life you've led, but dang it all, I wouldn't care about that. Not if you wouldn't. I ain't so all-fired purified myself."

Rose dragged in a long breath. "Oh, I know, Walter. And it isn't like I'm saying no, exactly. It's just that you've surprised me with your asking, and I'll have to think about it. Don't take that as a no."

He rose from the table. "Oh, I won't, Miss Rose. I won't take it as a no at all. I reckon I'd better make my rounds and see everything's locked up tight." He stopped, his face twisted in a grin. "Reckon what them folks coming out of the opry house thought when they saw the street filled with fighting, tussling upstanding citizens. Might have been a sight more interesting than that naughty play they'd been watching, you think?"

Rose laughed. "Indeed it might have been. A wonder how men can be so titillated by a play that parades around the same nonsense they're used to seeing in my place any Saturday night."

Walter chuckled and waved a good-bye.

With a sigh, she rose and locked up. No use in staying open. Everyone was in jail or home with their wives trying to stretch their earlier experiences into their own bedroom. She wondered briefly if Ben and Dessa were together, then shook her head at her own romantic notions.

She still missed Jarrad Lincolnshire, but Walter's proposal was something to think about. It might just be time for her to move on to another place, a whole new life, before she got too old to enjoy it. Walter was a kind man, and if she knew anything at all, she knew that a woman couldn't do any better than to snag a kind man.

Eleven

Early Sunday morning Dessa awoke in her own bed before dawn, a coverlet pulled over her fully clothed body, not knowing how she had gotten there. Her tongue was coated with the bitter taste of beer. For a moment she could recall nothing except that crazy fight in the street the night before. All those women, righteous and sinner alike, mixing it up in front of half the town. Despite the foul taste in her mouth, she grinned at the memory.

The rest came back in a flash as she sat up and reached for the water she kept on the nightstand. Ben touching her. Ben licking his thumb and wiping a smudge from her cheek, Ben lifting her to her feet and hugging her...holding her...and her holding him. Then nothing. A blank. What had happened? Had Ben...?

Of course he hadn't. She'd feel differently, wouldn't she? And besides, he wouldn't do something like that.

She decided to put off breakfast and take an early morning ride, and that's how she ended up at the livery stable long before anyone was up and about in the quiet streets.

No sidesaddle hung in the tack room. Then she remembered that a few days ago Rose had said that the girth had broken. It was probably at the leather shop being repaired. She lifted one of the western saddles from a stanchion along the wall. Unlike the lightweight English saddle she had grown used to in Kansas City, this one weighed almost more than she could heft.

To top it off, the Baron danced and snorted, refusing to let her come near him, and she ended up putting the saddle on Beauty instead. After studying the leather straps a moment, she threaded the cinch properly and pulled it tight around the animal's middle.

She had never ridden astride a horse, but could see no earthly good reason why a woman shouldn't do so if she wished. Feeling a strong animal between her legs couldn't be such a sin, could it? After she mounted, she saw that the stirrups were too long, she could barely reach them with pointed toes, so she slid off and adjusted them. Finally comfortably astride the long-legged mare—what would Mother and Father think of their properly brought up daughter mounting an animal like a man?—Dessa rode from the dark barn into the deserted street.

Beauty set a gentle pace, giving Dessa a chance to think. So much had changed in her life in such a short time. Oddly, that no longer made her sad. It was more like the way she felt after experiencing an especially poignant moment. Melancholy but assured that life offered more hope than sorrow. She had made new friends, Ben Poole among them; and of course Rose and Maggie. If she stayed here, there would be more.

Trust was important to her, and surprisingly she trusted Ben completely. He would never take advantage of her, just like last night when he carried her home, put her to bed, and left without so much as removing an article of clothing. She had been foolish to even think for a moment that he had taken any liberties. Realization of that trust produced a warm feeling next to her heart. She had experienced it with no one save her parents, most certainly not with men like Andrew. Look away and his hand shifted into a wandering mood.

Strange, when she thought of Andrew at all she compared him to Ben Poole.

Beauty kept to the main road leaving town, and she let the reins lie loosely in her gloved hand. The silvery dawn purpled, then glowed pinkly. A breeze blew down out of the mountains carrying the scent and touch of snow, and she breathed deeply of the damp sweetness. Oh, God, how lovely it was here, and how she hated to think of leaving. She had found her own paradise, quite by accident and under some pretty horrible circumstances, but nevertheless, her soul yearned to remain.

She tried to imagine the long winter, virginal snow piled high against the eaves to shut out the outside world, leaving her to deal with only her inner most murmurings. Her breath coming like clouds when she ventured outdoors, the clean air filling her lungs and making her skin tingle. And then, of course, there was Ben. He was as much a part of this place as that stand of stalwart pines up ahead.

The deep shadows beneath the trees brought to mind the mysterious but familiar man who had attended her mother and father's funeral. She was beginning to lose hope that she would ever know who that man was. At first she had thought that if she remained in town, he would one day approach, introduce himself. Explain why he had disappeared without speaking to her. But when that hadn't happened, the incident had begun to fade until she only thought of it at rare moments.

She came back to herself, halting her roaming thoughts. She had no idea where she was and had no desire to get lost in this immense country. The mare had steadfastly followed a little used trail and was moving along quite briskly, just as if she knew where she was going.

From the crest of the rise, Dessa spotted a house. A simple structure with clapboard walls and a long porch, it nestled snugly into a gentle south slope. There were a few chickens in the yard and wood-slatted pens out back. Long rays of sunlight broke across the meadow as the sun cleared the peaks and flashed on windowpanes.

Her mount slowed, walked leisurely into the yard and stopped without being bidden. She sat there a moment, puzzled. The mare knew where she was, obviously came here often.

Without any warning, two toddlers who looked to be the same age burst out the front door shouting with laughter, bare bottoms gleaming. Right behind them came a woman.

"Nathan, Jason, you come right back here this instant," she shouted, and made a swooping capture of both children. When she raised with one tucked firmly under each arm, she spied Dessa. "Oh, my. Hello. I didn't see you. Excuse these young heathens. I can't keep clothes on them."

Dessa smiled down at the woman. She couldn't remember ever seeing her in town. "Hello. I'm Dessa Fallon, and I seem to have let my horse lead me astray. Woolgathering."

The woman studied the black mare, a furrow between her eyes, then she, too, smiled. "Get on down and come have some coffee. I promise I'll put clothes on these two young'uns. My name's Sarah Woodridge. This here is Nathan." She jostled one of the boys. "This other'n is Jason, twins, and double trouble if ever there was any."

Dessa laughed and dismounted. She would enjoy taking coffee with this young woman, who appeared to be not much older than she herself. Looping the reins around a fence post, she followed Sarah up the steps and inside the neat small house.

"Set yourself there," Sarah said, motioning toward a rough-sawn wooden table with four chairs. "Coffee's on the stove. I'll just be a minute with these two."

She disappeared through a faded curtain hanging over a doorway that led from the larger main room, which appeared to serve as kitchen and living quarters. She returned quickly, trailed by the two boys, now clad in patched britches and faded shirts and acting quite shy of their visitor. They hung behind their mother, peeking out from behind her calico skirt.

Dessa winked and made faces at them, setting them both giggling. She saw no sign of a man, but he could be out hunting or working the fields.

"I don't get to town much, but I don't remember seeing you there," Sarah offered, and poured their coffee into mismatched cups.

"No, I've only been in Virginia City a short while." Dessa wondered if she should tell Sarah about her parents, but decided not to. That could wait until they were better acquainted.

"Well...is it...I mean, are you married or anything? How do you like Virginia? It's pretty primitive compared to..."

When Dessa realized the young woman wasn't going to finish the sentence, she said, "Oh, no, I'm not married. But I do love it here. It's so beautiful, the air is so heady and the mountains are breathtaking, not like the plains, so monotonous. Of course, some of Missouri is hilly, the Ozarks are quite lovely, but Kansas City is...well, it's busy and noisy and smelly."

"I'm from Philadelphia...so was my husband, Clete." Sarah abruptly looked away, stared out the kitchen window.

Dessa had the feeling she gazed not at the view but inward toward some sorrow. "He died," she said then, and brushed angrily at her eyes. "Would you like more coffee?"

Dessa lifted her half-full cup and sipped. "No, I'm fine." She waited a moment in reverence to Sarah's grief, then said, "The boys, they're darling. They must be good company for you, out here alone so far from town. I don't see how you can stay. I mean, I would think you'd go back to your people, or at least move to town."

Sarah's eyes grew dreamy. "Clete loved this place. We worked so hard proving it up. I'd feel like I was betraying him, walking away."

"But how can you do the work by yourself?"

Sarah shrugged. "The place is getting in pretty sorry shape, but I have some help."

Dessa nodded, not knowing what else to say. After all, she knew little of the woman's situation. There could be a man courting. She decided she had stayed long enough for her first visit, and rose.

Sarah popped out of her chair. "Oh, are you leaving so soon?"

"Yes, I'd like to get back and go to church. Perhaps I could come again at a better time?"

Sarah nodded her head and held out her hand. Dessa took it, noted the cracks and callouses in the skin. A tough life, this one. She admired Sarah's strength.

Before she could cross the room, the sound of horse's hooves pounded up in the yard, and a harried Ben Poole burst into the room without knocking.

"Ben," Sarah said, her face flushing with pleasure.

Dessa echoed her, but without the pleasure. "Ben?"

"Sarah? Dessa? I thought the mare…I mean you…had run away, then I saw her outside, but I couldn't…What are you doing out here, Dessa?"

Dessa was dumbstruck, for Sarah had gone to Ben and was standing beside him like he was her man, staring up into his face. Very pleased to see him, from the look of it. Ben continued to glare at Dessa, total confusion distorting his features.

"Ben?" Dessa said with a hint of demand in her query. She wanted to tell him to explain this situation, but felt speechless. It was really none of her business, she just wished it was, so she kept quiet.

"You know each other?" Sarah asked.

"And you know Dessa?" Ben asked her.

Both women replied at once. "We just met."

"Well, I…I guess…" Ben jerked off his hat, and at that moment Nathan and Jason raced in from the other room and locked themselves firmly around each of his legs, squealing and laughing.

Ben whooped and lifted them both in his arms. "Hey, there, you tadpoles."

Dessa watched the horseplay in total amazement. Ben tickled the boys and set them to giggling. He didn't look at Dessa again, but concentrated on playing with the twins.

"I think I'd better be getting back to town," Dessa stammered, and ran from the room before either of them could say a word.

She fumbled with the twisted reins, her fingers feeling thick and misbehaving. Finally she captured them and climbed on the dancing mare's back. It was no wonder the animal had known her way out here. Ben rode her here often, obviously. What in the world was going on anyway? Ben Poole and that woman who said her name was Sarah Woodridge, acting so cozy, and him playing with the twins like they were his very own. Was it possible they were?

That she had been totally fooled by the man disturbed her equilibrium. Surely Rose wouldn't have allowed such a deception. He could be their uncle or just a close friend of their dead father. Yet she sensed something was going on here beyond normal friendship, and she didn't like it one bit. Those two in there were just too lovey-dovey. Maybe Rose didn't know.

Dessa tapped at the horse's ribs with her heels and headed for town, anger and confusion gnarling her emotions in a tight ball.

She remained in her house all that day, seeing no one. She was so upset she didn't even attend church or meet Rose at the Continental House for breakfast, as had become her habit. Rose came by and banged hard on the door, but Dessa didn't answer.

Ben wanted to rush out after Dessa when she ran from Sarah's house, but with the twins in his arms and Sarah demanding to know what was going on, he could do nothing but listen to the sound of the black mare's hoof beats fade into the distance.

"Who is she, Ben?"

"Dessa Fallon."

Sarah tugged on his arm. "Silly, I know her name. Who is she to you, and why was she so upset? We were just having coffee and a visit. Why did she run off like she'd seen a ghost? I never have visitors, Ben."

Ben sighed at the familiar lament, then immediately felt guilty. He did a lot of that around Sarah, and it really wasn't her fault.

"Why was she here anyway?" Ben asked, and set the boys down to pour himself a cup of coffee.

"Said she was out riding and got lost, just rode up on the place by accident. Why?"

Ben gazed out the window across the meadow for a moment. Was that really the truth, or had Dessa followed him here earlier and returned to check up on him? He didn't know what to think, except that the look on her face told him she was hurt. He'd have to try to explain to her about Sarah and the twins. But how? How in God's name do you tell someone you care for that you're a killer?

Ben wasn't sure yet that what he felt for Dessa was love, for he had little experience in that realm, but he did know that he wanted to be with her, to touch her, to make her happy, to keep her safe. And he wasn't sure he could ever do that. It might be better to just let her believe what she wanted. She'd soon get over her disappointment in him, especially when she decided to go back to the city and stop playing her little games with her bumbling frontiersman.

Ben sipped at the hot coffee, his mind far from the small cabin. Then he noticed Sarah staring at him, and he smiled at her. "You feeling okay?"

She nodded, her slate-gray eyes morose. "What is she to you, Ben? She's so pretty and so smart. Did you hear the way she talks? All smooth and smart, like a lady. Not rough and dumb like me."

"You're not rough and dumb, Sarah. You know you're not."

"Well, Clete certainly didn't think so. He loved me and only me, even if I did live on the wrong side of town." Sarah sniffed and turned her gaze from Ben.

He tightened his lips and set down the empty cup. His heart ached when she spoke of her dead husband. He was responsible; it was his fault that Sarah had no one to care for her and the boys.

The horrible scene in town last spring played itself over and over in his mind, but he couldn't make it come out any way but the way it had truly happened.

Despite all of that, he couldn't force himself to love this woman. He couldn't take that final step and marry her because of his guilt. But he feared that one day he might give.

"Oh, Ben, I'm sorry," Sarah said, and threw her arms around him. "I love you, Ben. I don't mean to act that way. I do love you."

"I know you do," he said, and patted awkwardly at her back. How could he tell her that he didn't love her, that he never would, that all he could think of was that sprite of a girl who had rushed out of here with her green eyes afire?

Ben didn't know what he was going to do, but he was tired of being miserable over one woman or another. Maybe he'd just light out and go west to California. Leave both women and all his troubles behind.

Monday morning Dessa received another wire from the Cluney & Brown law firm in Kansas City, urging her to return before winter. Her presence, they insisted, was necessary whether she sold the business or not. Matters required her immediate attention if the Fallon stores were to survive the transition.

Considering what had happened out at Sarah Woodridge's the day before, there need be no further delay. If she had remained in Virginia City at all, it would have ultimately been because of her attraction to Ben Poole. All the other reasons were just rationalizations, after all. She had friends in Kansas City, people she'd known all her life. What had she been thinking, anyway, to even consider settling in this backward frontier town in the edge of nowhere? And all because of a man. Nonsense, utter and complete. There were plenty of men back home, and that's where she belonged.

She tucked the wire into her reticule and set out to find Rose. It wouldn't be an easy thing, leaving Rose and Maggie. She would miss them. Though she hated to admit it, she would miss Ben Poole the most. She hated giving up her dreams of a life that might have been theirs had things been different, but he had made such a fool of her, him and his teasing and leading her on. Playing hard to get just so she would want him even more. And all the time he had that woman on the side and two young'uns that for all she knew belonged to him. She had no idea how long Sarah's man had been dead.

She wanted to bust him one, just double up her fist and knock him a winding for what he'd done to her.

Rose didn't take well to Dessa's announcement that she was returning immediately to Kansas City. Wisely, Dessa mentioned nothing about Ben's part in her decision.

"Oh, I don't think that's a good idea, child. Bad enough you traveled alone coming here. You saw what happened, and the same goes for returning. You may have been hardheaded and spoiled enough to convince your parents it would be safe, but I know better."

"I have to go, Rose. I have obligations. My daddy's business was important to him. He worked very hard to make it what it was. I can't simply sit by while it falls apart."

"Then let someone go with you."

The two women sat on the chaise in the room Rose had lent Dessa when she first came to Virginia City. It had turned out to be Rose's private quarters away from the small cottage a few miles outside town where she lived—the cottage with the rose gardens where Rose went to relax and think calm thoughts when she could get away from the Golden Sun.

Dessa eyed Rose, wondering just what she had up her sleeve with the suggestion that someone accompany her to Kansas City.

"Who? Everyone has his own life here. I can't expect someone to just drop everything and go traipsing around with me. No, I'm not helpless." Her eyes teared and she wiped the moisture away angrily. "I have to learn to do things on my own. There isn't any choice."

"That's what you thought when those horrible men dragged you off that stagecoach. They could have killed you. It could happen again."

"Oh, Rose. Terrible things could happen to any of us, anytime. We can't go hiding out from them, being afraid to live because of them. Like Ben does."

Rose shot Dessa a harsh look. "What do you really know about what Ben does or why he does it?"

Dessa shrugged, sorry she'd said anything. It was none of her business anyway, though for a while she'd thought everything about Ben might someday be her business.

"You don't know the first thing about Ben and what motivates him."

Dessa squirmed. It was all she could do to keep from railing at this woman for what Ben had done. Rose was the closest thing to a mother he had, and Dessa should have known better than to criticize him to Rose. "I'm sorry, Rose. I didn't mean that. It's just that I wish…well, I wish things were different, but they aren't. And I must go. I simply must."

Rose stood, walked purposefully to her side. "Then Ben will go with you."

"He most certainly will not," Dessa sputtered. "Why in the world would he do that? And how can you even say he will without asking? And what makes you think I want him to go with me?"

"Calm down, child. Think about it a moment. You need someone to accompany you. Who better than Ben? You know you're safe with him. If it bothers you, offer to pay him. Make it a job."

"Ben would never accept such a job," Dessa said, and too late realized that with the statement she had allowed Rose to think she had capitulated. It really didn't matter, though. Ben would never agree to such a thing. Not in a thousand years.

She wiped at tears that surprised her in their suddenness. Why had he done this to her? And Rose thinking him nearly a saint.

"He'll be your bodyguard. Lots of people have them. It's not at all unusual." Rose chattered on, but Dessa shut out her words.

She tried to visualize Ben Poole in a drawing room in one of her friends' homes. She couldn't picture it, no more than she could picture him in her life in any other way. Not after what she'd seen this morning. It was impossible, utterly impossible.

Rose's words dragged her away from the wandering. "... we'll see to your place till you can come back. I'll be just fine."

Dessa rose and walked to the window. She peered down into the street below, unable to face her friend. "I'm not coming back," she finally said softly. The words cut a slice from her heart.

Rose was instantly at her side. "But my dear child, why ever not? I thought you liked it here. You talked about making a life here, not going back to all that big city hubbub. Here a woman's free, child. Why, we've even gotten the vote in Wyoming Territory. Up in South Pass City they've elected a female justice of the peace. Soon it will spread. Just think of it, Dessa.

"Think, child. Think. Think what it will be like to help build this country, to be a part of it. I wish I were young enough to see it happen, but you...you can do it. You and Ben."

"Ben? Ben doesn't want any part of me; he's just been playing with me. Oh, Rose, please stop it. Just don't talk to me about your precious Ben Poole anymore. He's ruined everything."

"Child, whatever's the matter? What has that young hellion done to you now? I warned him. I'll snatch him baldheaded if he's hurt you." Rose gathered Dessa against her bosom and patted her tenderly on the back. "Whatever it is, he just doesn't know any better. I'll straighten him out right now. Come, child, don't be so upset."

Dessa caught her breath and moved out of Rose's embrace. "I don't know what I'll eventually do, but for now, I have to return and I can't leave everything dangling here for someone else to handle. I fear I won't come back, once I leave; and I have to leave."

Rose took Dessa in her arms again, trying to comfort her but needing comfort herself, for she had pictured Ben and Dessa hand in hand, cutting a swath a mile wide across this virgin land. Doing something big and brave and wonderful that she was too old to accomplish herself. She had to convince Dessa to let Ben go with her to Kansas City, she simply had to. He would come back and he would bring Dessa with him. She wouldn't lose this child who had grown so dear to her heart.

"I'll wire Andrew, have him come out," Dessa said.

Rose pulled away, held the girl by her shoulders, and gazed deep into her eyes. "Andrew?" she asked dumbly. Who the hell was Andrew?

Dessa met her friend's gaze and nodded. "A friend, Rose. A good friend. Don't worry about me. Please don't fret so. I've enjoyed being here, but it's not real. It's a fantasy, and one I can't have. I'll arrange everything. Someone from back home can come out and accompany me. Ben needn't be bothered."

Noticing the destitute expression on Rose's face, Dessa put her arms around her. Unbidden, tears flowed down her cheeks while Rose hugged her so tightly she could hardly breathe.

Rose sent word to Walter Moohn that when Wiley Moss and Ben returned from their freighting run, he was to tell Ben she must see him immediately. It was nearly nine o'clock when he strode into the Golden Sun Saloon, his face a mask of fury.

She drew him a beer and he drank it without even saying hello first. Then he slammed the mug on the bar, wiped his mouth with a shirtsleeve, and said, "I quit."

"Quit? Quit what, Ben? Acting like a jackass?"

"I ain't acting like no jackass. I quit my job. I'm going to California."

"You're what?" Rose screeched so loud all the patrons shut up and gaped at her.

"I quit my damned job. You yourself said more than once I had no ambition, that I wasn't getting anywhere. Well, now I am. And I hope every blamed woman in the world is happy." He glared at her and shouted, "Give me another beer."

Rose blinked in surprise and filled his mug. "Ben Poole, don't you yell at me. Just settle yourself down, now, young man. What are you railing on about? It sure isn't a woman's fault you're in the fix you are."

"The hell it ain't. That young brat come sashaying into Virginia like her pretty little tail was on fire, wanting a little of this and a little of that from me. Playing like we were fated, or some such nonsense. And Sarah's worse, pulling at me all the time, and then you, Rose. All of you never leave me be."

"I'm sick of it all. So I quit my job and I'm leaving town."

He fired such a look of defiance at Rose she gasped. She'd never seen Ben act this way, and wasn't sure how to handle him.

Gathering her thoughts, she wiped at the spilled beer on the counter in front of him. It was obvious to Rose that Ben and Dessa were in love. All that was needed were a few nudges in the right direction, and they'd see their way through the mess young'uns always made of such a situation.

"Well, then, you can accompany Dessa back to Kansas City, seeing as how you no longer have a job," Rose said, and aimed her own defiant stare toward Ben.

"What? Haven't you been listening to a word I've said? I wouldn't go across the street for that stuck-up fancy flirt, much less travel all the way to that rotten city with her. Let her go alone, and good riddance."

"You don't mean that, Ben. You care for Dessa, and you blamed well know it. I'd think you'd be the last one to want her setting out on such a journey. Look what happened the last time she did that. You saw it for yourself, and now you stand there acting like a perfect fool. Those yahoos are still out there. Who's to say they won't do the same thing again?"

"Well, for sure not me. If they took such a notion in their head, I wouldn't be able to stop them. Besides, the stage has been left alone since that very day. I'd say they scooted right out of the country, what with the posse riding out every day for two weeks looking for them. Not a sound or sign from 'em tells me they're gone."

"Oh, well, mister know-it-all. I'm sure you're right and this country is perfectly safe for any young woman who wants to traipse around unattended. Just set her on the trail, let the Indians or outlaws or any drunken bum who takes a notion do what they please with her. That what you want?"

Ben clasped his large hands together on the bar and sighed. He felt himself losing this argument.

"You know it's not, Rose. But dadgummit, I don't want to go to Kansas City, or any other blasted city, for that matter. Why can't she just stay here? What put this notion into her head anyway?"

"Well, I guess you'll have to ask her that question yourself, because I don't understand it. From what little she'd say, it's something to do with you. What'd you do to her?"

"Damn it all, Rose. Damn it all."

But that was all Ben would say. Dessa would have stayed in Virginia if she hadn't seen him and Sarah together, and now she was leaving. It was clear why. If he gave in to Rose and went with Dessa, he'd be doing something out of his own feelings of guilt once again. When would he ever be able to do something just because he wanted to do it?

Rose picked up his empty mug and raised her brows. He shook his head no.

"I don't know," she said. "I've done everything I can to dissuade her, Ben. Only thing I can say is if you go with her, maybe you can make her come back."

Ben studied on that, knotting his fists together on the bar top. "She belongs in Kansas City, not here in this place. And I reckon if me going with her is what it takes to get her out of my life once and for all, then that's what I'll do.

"But Rose, I ain't bringing her back with me. And the sooner I can see her off that train and get myself headed back west, the better I'll feel. Then I reckon there'll be time enough for me to head for California." Ben hesitated a moment, seeing the despair on Rose's features.

"You and Walter ought to come along with me out West, Rose. Them women ain't gonna let up on you, and sooner or later the sheriff and lots of others in town are gonna have to side with them. Better you just up and leave before that happens."

Rose grew thoughtful. Maybe Ben was right, but she hated like the very devil to say good-bye to everyone, and most especially Dessa Fallon. Maggie and the girls might go to California with her, but losing Dessa would break her heart.

"Then I can tell Dessa you'll accompany her?"

"I'll tell her myself," Ben said, "right now, this minute. And we can have this whole thing over with, for good and for all."

Twelve

Dessa packed everything, leaving the contents of the chest in the bedroom until last. For a long while she sat cross-legged on the floor and held the forgotten, unopened package the sheriff had brought her soon after the funeral. She touched the knotted string tentatively.

She trembled, suddenly afraid without knowing why. What would she find in there? Opening it now when she was on the verge of returning to her old life but without her parents didn't seem wise. She simply could not bring herself to do so. Rationally, this was no time to open it anyway. Perhaps when she was safely back in the home of her childhood, she would spread the contents out on her bed and finger through them, remember the times she wanted never to forget, before the horror of her parents' death. What few precious possessions had her mother chosen to save for her in those last terrible moments when she realized she was about to die? Or had she simply panicked and tossed out the first thing she laid her hands on?

Dessa shook away the horrid images that rapped at her consciousness. She would open the package at home in her own room cradled by the familiarity of her own bed, let the tears of grief flow surrounded by all that had become so soothing in her life.

For now, she refused to begin a long, hard trip emotionally distraught. It was bad enough the way she felt about Ben, without adding reminders of her earlier loss.

Someone banged loudly on the door. She leaped to her feet, dropped the package in her trunk, and hurried through the parlor. Whoever could that be this late at night?

Leaning her cheek against the wood, she called, "Who is it?"

"Me, Ben Poole."

Dessa smacked the flat of her hand on, the door." Go away."

"Open the door, Dessa. Rose sent me."

'Tell me what she wants. I'm not letting you in."

"Come on, Dessa. I won't yell our business out here on the street for everyone to hear. Just open the door. This won't take but a minute. What's wrong, are you afraid of me?"

Dessa grabbed the key from its nail, unlocked the door, and threw it open. "I'm not afraid of you, Ben Poole, I'd just rather not see you again. Tell me your business from right there. You don't need to come in."

And then she raised her eyes to his. Such a feeling of pending loss swept over her that she swayed with the enormity of it, fingers pinching at the frame to hold herself up.

Ben took a tentative step. "Are you sick or something?"

The lamplight behind her threw her features in shadow. He knew every inch of that lovely face, and he fought the urge to trace its angular smoothness with the tips of his fingers, feel the warmth of her flesh against his own. She was very angry with him, and with good reason, but he refused to admit that aloud. Instead he just asked again, "You okay?"

She tightened her lips. "I'm fine. What did you want?"

Ben noticed she left the door open wide and he took another step toward her as he spoke. "Not me. Rose."

"Okay, what did Rose want?"

"She asked me to tell you that I will be able to take the job of accompanying you to Kansas City." He grinned despite himself. "Accompanying, that's what she said. Not my word."

"Oh, I know it's not your word." She was ashamed that her voice dripped with sarcasm and tried again, softening the tone. "Why would you want to go with me anyway? I'm going to wire a friend to come out and make the return trip with me."

"That'll take a while. I could have you home in a few days, save you waiting on him." He stared down at his boots a moment. "Who is he, some back East dandy? You think he could protect you if those yahoos take it into their heads to hit the stage again?"

"Oh, and you could? Besides, Andrew's not a dandy. He's an amateur boxer, among other things."

"Well, good, he could jump out of that stage and challenge them to a boxing match. Get hisself shot, is what he'd get."

"Ben, please. What good is this going to do?"

"To tell you the truth, I don't know. Rose talks a good argument. I think if we just do what she wants and get it over with, we'll both be happier, and she durn tooting will be. It don't hurt to please Rose. She's a good woman, and she loves us both."

Taken aback by the declaration and his use of the word us, as if the two of them somehow belonged together, she took another step backward. He went on in but left the door ajar behind him.

His talk about love momentarily overpowered her ability to say anything. Then she remembered the way Sarah Woodridge hung on him. No woman did that without just cause.

She cocked her head at Ben smartly. "And just what will your little pretty do without you while you're gone?"

"My little pretty?" He was perplexed for a moment, then realized who she was talking about. "Sarah is not my little pretty. Aw, hell, I'm sick to death of all this. Just get your things together. I'll get us tickets on the stage in the morning and we can get this over with. You'll be back where you belong, and I can go on to California with a clear conscience."

"California? You're going to California?" Something inside her plunged into awful darkness. She wondered why she cared, wondered further why she asked.

"Yes'm, I am. Just as soon as I get you back where you belong."

"Why do you keep saying that? Where I belong. I belong where I want to be. I suppose Sarah's going with you?"

"That's not your business. I'd appreciate it if you would be ready. The stage usually pulls in before noon. It'll only be here an hour or so."

She gave up. All she wanted was out of this place in the quickest way possible, and Ben's offer, even though under pressure from Rose, seemed the most sensible.

With a sigh, she said, "I'll be ready. Will you send someone for my trunk? It's heavy."

"I'll come get it."

"Good night, then."

"To you, too." He turned and left, and she slammed the door so hard it shook the walls of the little house.

Sometime during the night a storm hit, wind and rain rattling at the roof over Dessa's head. But it didn't awaken her, for she hadn't been asleep. Visions of Ben Poole's angry face remained in her thoughts. The hard set to his mouth, the frosty glaze of those blue eyes had bespoken a fury she had never seen in him before. What had upset him so? If anyone should have been angry, it was her. But it was all over now, the ridiculous desire that he might love her, the dreams of making a life with him. All over, and probably to the good.

Better an uneventful life with Andrew or someone like him than a bare existence with Ben Poole, who was nothing more than a frontier savage. She was glad he was coming with her, but dreaded making the trip with him. It would be very difficult to look into his eyes every day and deny the way she felt. Cover up the shivers of excitement when he touched her, hide the desire that burned inside. She would have to feed her own anger and his to make the trip bearable.

She had lost her parents to this ferocious land, and now she was losing Ben Poole, and there seemed nothing she could do about it. She finally fell asleep to the sound of rain on the roof, and dreamed of a furtive stranger, always just out of reach of her probing search. She had almost forgotten the man in the cemetery, and now that she was leaving, he came back to haunt her, to make her wonder who he could be. It was too late, though, and she would probably never know who he was. She was going home.

Velda Brotherton writes from her home perched on the side of a mountain against the Ozark National Forest. Branded as *Sexy, Dark and Gritty,* her work embraces the lives of gutsy women and heroes who are strong enough to deserve them. After a stint writing for a New York publisher, she has settled comfortably in with small publishers to produce novels in several genres.

Facebook: Author Velda Brotherton
Twitter: @veldabrotherton
www.veldabrotherton.com

www.ingramcontent.com/pod-product-compliance
Lightning Source LLC
Chambersburg PA
CBHW05094212 0626
46552CB00001B/337